Nguen Lo watched the rain turning his fields into a sea of mud. The monkey was stewing in the pot with turnips, onions, hot Vietnamese chilies and a generous amount of nuc mam. He smiled at his children playing on the raised bamboo floor of the simple hut. Rain came in the cooking hole, spattering on the hot coals and cast iron.

The dampness bothered his ankles and knee. The knee had never properly healed after it shattered on the bulkhead of his flaming A6 Intruder. The ankles had both been smashed with the butt of an old .03 Springfield, after he had tried to escape from the reeducation camp. Both events were a lifetime ago.

He had all but forgotten Lt. J.G. Charles Everett Montgomery, USN.

He could not remember the faces of his parents, or even his EWO, who had not survived the bailout over the North Vietnamese canopy. He was Nguen Lo, loyal citizen of the DEMOCRATIC PEOPLES REPUBLIC OF VIETNAM. He gave his wife a kiss and a pat on her gently swollen abdomen. *I should have a son before harvcst,* he thought.

Hc found a place at the communal pot. Incense was burning at the base of the smiling Budda. The family nodded their heads respectfully in his direction, in thanks for the meal.

P.O.W.

by

Gil Hash

Commonwealth
Publications

A Commonwealth Publications Paperback
P.O.W.

This edition published 1995
by Commonwealth Publications
9764 - 45th Avenue,
Edmonton, AB, CANADA T6E 5C5

ISBN: 1-896329-01-2

Printed in Canada

Cover Illustration by
Scott Taylor

Dedicated to the memory of my grandfather,
Joseph A. Saly who taught me the
value of the written word

Chapter One

1930 EST 19 July
VFW Hall, Crandal, Michigan

John Murphy watched his wife of eighteen years, as she weaved through the small crowd of friends and well wishers. They had gathered at the Crandal VFW to celebrate John's fifth decade on the planet. He recalled it had been over twenty years since he had returned to the world. She was still a damn fine looking woman after eighteen years, three children, countless family emergencies, and minor tragedies. Since the nightmares ended almost ten years ago, barring a few notable exceptions, John L. Murphy, Sgt. Major, Army of the United States, Special Forces (ABN) (Retired), only thought about *the Nam* when he was with his buddies at the VFW. Those were mostly thoughts of tight friends, missions accomplished, lush green tropics, the wonderful mountain tribes, and that particular rush of surging adrenaline and testosterone. He knew he would never be that alive again!

He was happy with his job, his wife, his kids, and his life in rural northern Michigan.

His eyes fell on the POW/MIA flag on the post wall and he was profoundly saddened – that whole thing is most certainly FUBAR!

"Earth calling John," said a melodious voice in

his ear. He slipped an arm around his warm, supple spouse.

"Hi Babe, REALLY LOVE YOU" , he said into the sweet smell of her hair.

"Drinks for the house," the Sargent Major bellowed.

2130 PST, 18 July
Columbia, Oregon

"Working fire, give me a second alarm," Battalion Chief Mike Roberts commanded into his microphone as he rounded the corner of a posh, residential area overlooking the Columbia River. He could see the dark puffs of smoke suck in and out of the closed, two story dwelling. Mike knew, a little oxygen would release the red dragon, to devour all within striking distance. His men expertly positioned the engine, snorkel, ladder truck, and rescue wagon. They used a hydrant on the far corner, downwind of the blaze.

He has always viewed fire-fighting as combat. Over the years this attitude has served him well. He had taken wounds and casualties, but he had survived, as had most of his men.

Late for supper again, he thought. Mike smiled as he thought of Shirley carefully saran-wrapping everything for the microwave. With the boys at college, she'd wait for Mike to come home to eat. She always had. Just as she had waited that dark thirteen months in '68-'69 when Mike Roberts had been with the 3/3 Recon, USMC – LONG AGO AND FAR AWAY – GOT A FIRE TO FIGHT!

0400 MST, 19 July
Hotel Dieu Emergency Department,

El Paso, Texas
Four a.m., two more hours and his emergency room shift would be over, *wonder how the M.I. is doing?* thought Dr. David Reynolds. *This damn tendon keeps retracting.* He gripped one end of the extensor superficialis with a pair of mouse-tooth hemostats. He then managed to sink the razor sharp P3 needle into each side, affecting a figure eight stitch, and drawing the ends together.

His patient was drunk. He had punched out the windshield of someone who had cast reflections on the moral turpitude of a local bar fly. The patient was dressed in jeans and T-shirt, emblazoned with the likeness of M.C. Hammer. He was twenty to twenty-one years old. The age when young men feel they can whip mountain lions. Dr. Reynolds's mind wandered to the faces of the other young men he had labored over. They also felt they could whip mountain lions, machine guns, land mines, and other explosive ordinance – they were wrong.

"Another pack of 4-0 Vicryl," he asked the soft young nurse. He had been seeing her ever since Barbara had packed up the kids and moved out. He could see her almond eyes smiling over the surgical mask. He inhaled her perfume, and thought of that firm golden backside.

0400 EST, 19 July
Grand Boulevard, Detroit, Michigan
Despite the hour, the streets' of Detroit were crowded. Hustlers, pimps, prostitutes, addicts, drug dealers, and those unable to escape the cesspool, went about their nightly duties. Sgt. Wade Washington swung the cruiser over, to see exactly

why the skinny young hooker was being beaten this particular night.

"Yo Bro," said the tall black in sharkskin suit, alligator cowboy boots, and huge eighteen carat gold African continent, suspended from his neck by a chain. A chain sufficient to hold a charging Doberman. "Back-off Juice," warned Washington. He slipped his baton into the ring at his belt, while exiting the patrol car. He wondered how much good his "Second Chance" vest would really do him, here in Indian country.

Once the family dispute had been resolved, and the skinny hooker had resumed her appointed rounds, Sgt. Washington checked out at a Dunkin Donuts for bad coffee and greasy fried dough. "Need to work on this gut," he told himself as he ordered two more jelly-filled. Didn't seem to matter much, since his wife and daughter had died in a house fire set during Devil's Night last Halloween.

1900 Local, 19 July
Quang Tri Province, Democratic Peoples Republic of Vietnam

"Have to get the cattle in quickly," said the tall, tanned man. He called to his wife and children, in rapid-fire Vietnamese, as the monsoon swept into the small village in Quang Tri province. His large, boney wrist and chiseled face seemed slightly incongruous among the short, round faced peasants. But what was most striking was his ice blue eyes.

0400 EST, 19 July
Washington, District of Columbia, USA

The Washington Monument was stark against the night sky as the limousine snaked through the sparsely populated streets toward Pennsylvania Avenue. Several men were huddled around a burning barrel. A brown paper bag was making the journey from lip to lip. Some of the men wore faded field jackets bearing shoulder patches from a long forgotten war. DIA agent Judd Carmicheal held the manila folder with the red-slashed border in his lap. The eyes only seal had been broken. He was trying to digest the latest papers from the newly formed Unified Eurasian Republics.

Judd had liberated French Foreign Legionnaires, taken at the fall of Dien Bien Phu, while he was operating with Recon Team Cobra, MACV-SOG. They were running cross the fence missions. This ticking time bomb he held in his lap was more dangerous than any article in the formidable U.S. armory.

He was enroute for a meeting in the ultra-secret War-Room. The president, the Joint Chiefs of Staff, and the heads of all security/intelligence agencies would be there, including his own boss Richard A. Markam. It seemed cold for D.C. in July!

Chapter Two

0400 EST, 19 July
The White House, Washington, D.C.

Even though the Marine in full dress blues, recognized Judd Carmicheal on sight. The DIA Special Agent in Charge, Atlantic Region, U.S. and Asian Affairs, showed his laminated I.D., and matched his palm with the laser sensor. This before a soft buzz opened the three feet homogeneous steel door leading to the Command and Control room of the most powerful nation on Earth. Judd knew it was swept for electronic surveillance weekly, and before every high level conference. He also knew it was virtually impenetrable, and would withstand most nuclear detonations. The Marine, though armed, was mostly window dressing. The real security measures, defensive and offensive, were very sophisticated, high tech., computer operated with multiple systems back-up.

Around the table was an awesome display of top brass, spit and polish, and a dazzling array of multicolored service ribbons.

Despite the hour, and suddenness of the meeting, the Joint Chiefs were turned out in full Class A uniforms, bespeaking of long and distinguished military careers. Directors of the FBI, CIA, DIA, NSC, and most of the bureaucratic alphabet were represented. They were all in well-tailored mufti. Carefully cut to conceal the effects of age and dietary indiscretions. Note pads, pens, and steaming cups of coffee were precisely placed in front of each participant.

At the head of the table, if a round table can have a head, sat a short, balding man in a rumpled suit. The only distinguishing article of attire was a small, enameled, sky blue rosette with a scattering of small white stars affixed to his lapel. This was the Commander in Chief, Hiram Caldwell, PRESIDENT OF THE UNITED STATES OF AMERICA.

The President rose and motioned Judd to a seat, to the right of Richard Markam. As the P.U.S. sat, he folded his small hands on the mahogany surface and said, in a quiet, yet surprisingly powerful voice, "So, Mr. Carmicheal, tell us what you have."

Judd Carmicheal, ex-Special Forces, Airborne Ranger, veteran of Laos, Vietnam and numerous covert missions and now DIA/SAC, had cotton mouth. His voice seemed to constrict in his throat, "Mr. President, we have confirmation from the Soviet Uni –, excuse me, the Unified Eurasian Republics that there are live Americans in the Democratic Peoples Republic of Vietnam."

The faces around the table were not stunned nor amazed. There had been occasional sightings since the fall of Saigon. All had "proved unfounded" by the very men gathered at this meeting. There had also been a number of cruel hoaxes victimizing family members who had never given up hope.

The President spoke, "You are aware that it has been official policy for some time that live POW/MIAs do not exist anywhere in Southeast Asia."

Judd started to speak but his boss interrupted, "Mr. President, several representatives of the UER have come forward with such claims, in an obvious attempt to elicit U.S. economic support."

Pure bureaucratic bullshit! thought Carmicheal.

"Judd, you know if there were any chance of even one American being alive in Vietnam, I would spend the full resources of this country to get him back. But you also know how many times these sightings have proven false. Even Yeltsin's claim was proven to be pure fantasy."

Each of the Joint Chiefs expressed similar doubts. The strongest disagreement came from an Air Force four star, who himself had over four years in Ho Loa Prison. "It's just not possible. I wish it were, believe me!"

Judd Carmicheal passed the file which contained fuzzy black and white photos of tall males of uncertain nationality, refugee statements, photostats of Democratic Peoples Republic of Vietnam prison records, and official correspondence between the DPRV and the USSR/UER regarding current status of "capitalist war criminals", some were dated this year.

Clinton Murray, Director of the CIA, studied the file then spoke, "Mr. President, we have in-country assets who can check this out, but I strongly advise against any provocative action or statements at this point in time."

Thomas Darrow, National Security Advisor, rose and addressed the room, "I see this as another attempt by the DPRV to extort the funds promised by Kissinger at the Paris Peace Accord. Several administrations have steadfastly refused to pay the gooks a dime. The French ransomed their POWs from Vietnam, and I don't see us doing the same thing. We are steadily receiving remains, and I think that is the best we can hope for. We cannot and will not find live Americans – that is policy!"

President Caldwell spoke. "Mr. Murray, your agency, with the assistance of Mr. Markam and his agency, is directed to ascertain the validity of any such claims and sightings. Then to report back to this body within ninety calendar days. You will have the full support of the executive office. Gentlemen, thank you." He rose and exited the enclave.

Richard Markam told Judd, "Mr. Carmicheal, you will submit the file with your written report to Mr. Murray. You will not be further involved in this particular investigation. Thank you for your assistance." Before Judd could reply the DIA Director rose and left the room. As Judd tossed the file toward the Director, and eight by ten fuzzy photo, dated less than thirty days ago, slipped out. It showed a tall, tanned male standing by a hut with an Oriental woman and two children. It was obviously taken with a powerful telephoto lens. "You'll get my report through channels," said Judd as he stalked out of the War-Room.

0630 EST, 19 July
BUDS, Little Creek, Virginia

Sr. Chief Petty Officer Harrison D. Chvostek, USN SEAL Team Six, watched the latest training platoon, soon to graduate BUDS, complete the confidence course. They plunged into the water for the five mile swim.

As Team Chief of the U.S. Navy's ultra secret counter-terrorist, rapid deployment/counter-insurgency team, he was always on the lookout for potential new team members. He had a stack of "201" files on the desk in front of him. Soon this would be someone else's job. On "nine September", Sr. Chief Chvostek, USN, was to pull the pin, and become Mr. Chvostek of Lahina, Maui. He had put over thirty thousand hard saved dollars into the Dive/Bait/Charter service his father owned. The new boats and equipment had really increased business. His attractive young wife at the front desk helped also. *Yep, it's Miller time,* he thought.

Harrison D. Chvostek's career had begun at the Bay of Pigs, continued through Laos, Cambodia, Vietnam, Grenada, Panama and Iraq, with side trips to Iran, France and Germany.

Through Navy and civilian courses, "Harry" had finished high school and earned a Bachelor's of Science in Advanced Computer Skills.

2300 EST, 19 July
Georgetown, Virginia

Judd Carmicheal pulled into the winding driveway of the Georgetown home. As he hit the garage door opener, he saw the kitchen light come on. Cindy would be waiting up. He sat in the car trying to decide how much he could share with his wife of five years. He wanted to talk to her, to express his frustration, doubts, fears, and concerns. She was wife number three, probably the best yet.

One had left when he was held in the jungle camps. One had left while he was in Teheran, as an in-country asset, during Operation Rice Bowl. He'd been a "chairborne trooper" all of this marriage.

Cindy was a Washington lobbyist for a large

defense contractor. Judd still found the dichotomy fascinating: Cindy Carmicheal was a stunning brunette with coal-black eyes and swimsuit model body who lobbied for the most vicious of devices known to modern man.

"Hi handsome," Cindy said as her lips brushed his ear through the open car window. It pulled him back from his reverie. She was wearing the black teddy he had bought her last Christmas. She had a "Cuervo 1800" in a frosty glass in each hand.

"Boy, do I need that, and this," Judd said. He stepped out of the car. He took his drink in one hand and his wife's nicely rounded rump in the other. She teased his tongue as their lips met.

"Hard day," she giggled into his mouth. Her hand sought his swelling crotch. "Ummm," he replied.

Since both Judd's children now lived with their mother, they had the luxury of the house to themselves. Cindy began undressing her spouse, nibbling and teasing as she removed his suit jacket and tie. She gently lowered the Baretta, M-9, semiautomatic pistol, nestled in its padded shoulder holster, to the garage floor. Cindy then led her husband to the small office, she maintained off the garage, she used as a work space and tax deduction.

The office was dominated by a large couch her mother had given her many years ago. She giggled, it was on this very couch in Bloomington, Indiana, were, at the tender age of sweet sixteen, she had been deflowered by a gangly college freshman.

Their lovemaking was intense and fiery. Judd needed her, especially tonight.

0800 EST, 20 July
Georgetown, Virginia

Sunday morning came gently into the Carmicheal house. Sunlight streaming through Cindy's office window, and jays calling. She slipped on a trench coat, from the garage coat closet, and retrieved the Sunday Times, and Saturday's mail. The preprogrammed "Mr. Coffee" had finished perking. Mrs. Carmicheal brought two steaming mugs of Kona coffee laced liberally with Kahlua.

Judd sipped his coffee and went through the mail—bill, bill, bill, plea from the University of Washington Alumni Association, and a "Static Line". He read the airborne fraternity newspaper first. A quarter page advertisement caught his eye—"Special Forces Association Twentieth Reunion, Five August, Fayetteville, North Carolina".

Judd had not taken a vacation from the Agency since his honeymoon five years ago. He doubted Cindy would want to go.

Over breakfast Cindy told him, "I think you should go." He had not discussed his early morning White House briefing, and Cindy had learned not to ask.

He felt the need to talk about Nam, and POW/MIAs in particular, but to who?

It might do him good to relax and swap war stories with the guys from Group. They were a unique breed of warrior.

0600 MST, 20 July
"Rocking 'T' Ranch", outside Billings, Montana

Chad Tanner had been born Cecil Cedrick Tanner III, esq. in Sheffield, England. (This was also the home of the Sykes-Fairborne fighting stiletto of WW II fame.) After his service with Her Majesty's Special Air Service, and near fatal wounds received in the Falkland Islands, he had immigrated to the U.S. of A. He bought this twenty thousand acre cattle ranch in the Big Sky country. The purchase was thanks to the somewhat timely demise of Sir Cecil Cedric Tanner II, while engaged in a little extra-curricular hanky-panky with the upstairs maid. "Old boy died in the saddle, so to speak," Chad always quipped.

The ranch had prospered. The discovery of a huge oil deposit, black gold, made Chad Tanner one of the richest men in Montana; a state with stiff competition for that title.

A few wise ventures on Wall Street had elevated him to one of the wealthiest men in America, and possible the world. Though he was probably edged out by the camel jockeys.

Even though it was more efficiently done by helicopter, and four-wheeler, it gave him a good feeling to "ride fence" across the rolling expanse he called, "Tequila Sunrise". It was officially recorded as the "Rocking 'T'", with the Montana Bureau of Brands Registration in Billings.

As he rode, he thought about the upcoming convention in Fayetteville. He decided it would be a good break from the business of ranching, and managing a financial empire.

Terry, his bride of fourteen years was in New York, shopping, and he was sure she would not mind, or even miss his absence.

His son, Chad, not Cecil, was a Plebe at West Point. His daughter, Amanda, was a Midshipman at Annapolis. He was not looking forward to the next Army/Navy game. Both appointments had been secured with the help of the "Senator from the Great State of Montana". The Senator was impressed with Chad's money, and his Victoria Cross. Both children had always been exceptional students and varsity athletes.

Chad couldn't quite decide when it was that Terry had slipped out of his bed, and his life. He knew that neither one of them could afford to leave the marriage.

Might do me good to hoist a pint with the bloody yanks in their green beanies, he thought, as his bay mare ambled on down toward the main house. A lone eagle soared overhead searching for a careless rabbit or prairie dog. A cool breeze wafted across the reservoir, carrying the sweet smell of sage. *It seems cold for July,* he thought.

1930 EST, 21 July
Detroit, Michigan

Sgt. Wade Washington had gotten a notice, from the Detroit Police Officer's Association, reminding him that, according to union contract with the city: "combined time off" was a use it or lose it proposition. The DPOA saw CTO as earned dollars lost, and strongly encouraged it's ten thousand plus members to take their vacation, sick and personal leave days in a timely fashion.

The SFA reunion notice had been lying on the battered coffee table, along with multiple half-eaten T.V. dinners and empty generic beer cans, for over a week. Wade decided he might as well go. It had been years since he'd seen Fayetteville, or any of his long-lost soulmates.

The apartment was too damn empty and lonely

anyway. Even that useless cat has long since left for more hospitable digs.

1830 EST, 22 July
VFW Hall, Crandal, Michigan
"Hey, SarntMajor, you going to Group reunion?" asked Carl Simmons, a young trooper with the Michigan National Guard, and "Desert Storm" veteran, who read the "Static Line" religiously.

"Dunno, Christine says I should," as he downed another 1800.

0800 EST, 22 July
BUDS, Little Creek, Virginia
Senior Chief Petty Officer Chvostek filled out the Assignment Related Education and Leave Request carefully. He knew a clerk-typist would have to enter all the information, correctly, in the Team Six roster and duty status. He figured the SFA reunion would be the last time he'd see most of those guys. He also knew, they would throw him one hell of a retirement party.

1930 PST, 22 July
Columbia, Oregon
"You really should go Mike, I'll go to Seattle and see my mother. It'll be good for you. You haven't seen some of those guys in twenty years. Besides, you always get pumped up when one of your airborne buddies comes around."

Shirley had already filled out the registration, and attached a check.

1600 MST, 22 July
Medical Staff Lounge, Hotel Dieu Hospital, El

Paso, Texas

"Current Concepts in Emergency Medicine", read the ACEP announcement, "July 30 to August 2, Duke University School of Medicine, Durham, North Carolina".

Dr. Reynolds knew the twenty year reunion of the Special Forces Association was August fifth to eighth in Fayetteville. He figured the Chief of Medical Staff would give him time off if he arranged coverage now.

He pulled out his battered American Express card and reached for the phone. He knew any day Karl Mauldin would call to tell him to, "leave home without it," but today it was still valid.

Chapter Three

0930 EST, 22 July
Defense Intelligence Agency,
Washington, D.C.

Judd Carmicheal was sitting at his desk bitterly completing his report to the CIA, when the private line on his desk rang. "Carmicheal," he answered tersely.

"Judd, this is Hiram Caldwell."

Judd unconsciously rose to his feet and assumed a military brace, "Yes Sir, Mr. President."

"Is this a secure line?" asked the President.

"Probably not Mr. President," replied Carmicheal.

"Can you swing by the House Athletic Club around eight tonight, we'll have a sweat?" asked the President.

"Uh sure, I mean YES SIR I'll be there," responded Carmicheal.

Judd hung up the receiver and sat back in his chair. *Now what the hell was that all about?* he thought.

1954 EST, 22 July
The White House Athletic Club
1600 Pennsylvania Ave. , Washington, D.C.

When Judd Carmicheal arrived at the Club, the

only persons in evidence were half-a-dozen, tall, crewcut young men in dark suits, with thin, plain ties and crisp white shirts. Occasionally speaking into their left sleeve, they were otherwise silent and unsmiling.

"I'm Judd Carmicheal of the DIA," he told the burly centurion at the door of the executive club, as he produced his credentials. The Secret Service agent studied the laminated plastic I.D., and compared the photo to the man standing before him. Finally, he nodded curtly and held the door open for the SAX, "Please proceed directly to the sauna, sir."

The agent in the changing room did not move or speak as Judd shed his clothes. Judd placed his suit and shoulder holster in the nearest locker, pinning the numbered key to his towel. Locking his weapon and possessions seemed superfluous in this setting.

Judd saw steam seeping from under the cedar door, and the sulking monolith held his palm in that general direction.

The steam was so thick, visibility was about six inches, but he found a bench and sat down. The wood was rough and hot against his bare buttocks.

"How are you doing Judd?' came a voice from the steam. He recognized it as belonging to the chief executive.

"Mr. President, exactly what is this all about?"

The answer came slow and deliberate, "I've read your refugee sightings and eye witness reports, examined your documents, cross referenced them with military records, and attempted verification. You may not be aware of it , but we have assets under deep cover in most of the communist controlled countries."

Judd nodded in the steam, even though the President could not see the affirmation.

"I think there ARE live Americans in Southeast Asia, and perhaps Russia also. I also think the CIA, and the DIA are going to prove they are not! I want you to bring them home!"

J.D. Carmicheal, long time soldier, long time DIA agent, accustomed to receiving and executing orders, sat silently. Finally he found his voice.

"You want the Agency to investigate this?" he asked.

The President moved closer, there was a surrealism to the balding head suspended in the steam, almost a divine presence.

"I want you to resign from the DIA to investigate this. This needs to be a civilian investigation," said the President.

"But how," Judd stammered. He was interrupted again by the man who had earned the Congressional Medal of Honor on a frozen reservoir in Korea.

"You will investigate, and ascertain the presence or absence of live American POW/MIAs, and execute a rescue mission if necessary. You and I will heal a festering wound, on the people of this country, that has been left open too long. When it's over, if you survive, and if you still want to return to the Agency, you will do so without loss of pay, benefits or seniority. Hell, do this, and live, and I'll make you Director of the damn DIA, or any other cabinet post you like."

President Hiram Caldwell rose, threw more cold water on the hot coals; his face disappeared in a suffocating cloud of steam.

"You will report only to me. Finances, contacts, equipment, and intelligence will be arranged and provided by me," commanded the disembodied voice.

"You will not discuss this with any government agency or organization. Nor will you involve any government employees, U.S. military personnel or installations.

You will not use U.S. military equipment or resources. You will however, have complete access to all personnel records, live sighting reports and official and unofficial documents. I will give you a back door access code. Inquires have to remain non-traceable," advised the President.

"You will have full authority, up to and including armed intervention. However, should you, or any member of your team be killed or captured, this office will disavow any knowledge of your mission. This will be strictly a private citizen venture."

Judd could almost hear the theme music from "Mission Impossible" as he was trying to digest the presidential dictum.

"With all due respect, Mr. President, I haven't accepted the mission."

Hiram Caldwell leaned forward and placed his small, surprisingly delicate hand on Judd's shoulder,

"I've read your file from VMA through DIA, you'll do it, and you'll do it well."

Judd noticed the President had extended his right hand through the miasma. Judd shook it firmly, and his Commander-in-Chief was gone into the steam. The door closed with a solid thunk behind the leader of the free world.

Judd Carmicheal stayed in the sauna. He was trying to organize the kaleidoscope of thoughts, ideas, emotions, and previous missions into a homogenous plan.

"I guess I accept the mission Mr. President," he said to the empty cedar vault.

Chapter Four

2100 EST, 4 August
Fayetteville Holiday Inn, North Carolina
"Welcome Special Forces Association," proclaimed the reader board at the convention center. It was just moments from the huge Ft. Bragg/Pope military complex.

Most of the arriving members had been stationed at the home of the 82nd. Airborne, and Special Forces. Most knew Fayetteville intimately.

It was also the home of "Delta Detachment", the U.S. Army Special Forces' ultra secret, counter-terrorist unit, stationed in a remote corner of the complex, formerly known as Camp McCall, now known simply as "The Ranch".

The bar was beginning to look like a soldier of fortune watering hole, as middle-aged men arrived wearing bits and pieces of camouflage fatigues, now known as BDUs.

There were a few battered berets of forest green, black and maroon. They were greeting old friends, and trying to find places at the rapidly filling bar. A few were missing various extremities. Some with the distinctive facial disfiguration associated with explosive trauma.

The sense of camaraderie was as intoxicating as the ethanol. Not only had these men made the journey, they had returned to an ungrateful nation, and gone out again. Simply because that same nation had asked them to do so. The pride was in the satisfaction that they had done a job only a few could have done.

They were not Rambo, Terminator, or Superman. They were men who had been highly trained, and highly motivated – with a sense of pride, elitism, patriotism and mission. They had done everything their country had asked, and more.

2145 EST, 4 August
room 2313, Holiday Inn, Fayetteville, N.C.

"Oh Ruuuuby, don't take your love to town," pleaded a soulful baritone on 107.5 Fayetteville Country Music, as Judd carved a piece of ripe lime from his Cuervo Gold using his SEAR knife.

The knife had been handmade, and given to him years ago by a buddy from Group – Al Mar. The micarta wood handle was as scarred and beaten as Judd's seamed, leathery countenance. The tool/weapon had certainly performed more ominous chores in it's long and colorful life. Fortunately for national security, it, like it's owner could not relate those tales.

Judd was debating going down to the bar. The letter of resignation from the DIA lay on the desk, folded neatly and addressed to the attention of: Richard A. Markam, Director.

Judd had promised Cindy he would not mail it until he returned from the reunion. He wondered if she could weather a mysterious disappearance. Cindy had long ago learned not to ask where, when, or why.

Over the years his other wives and assundry

lovers, had found more stable, predictable mates.

Judd knew that this was one last mission he must accomplish. A plan was forming in his fertile mind; fed and watered by the special ops climate, and a little tequila.

1830 EST, 4 August
Ramada Inn, Durham, North Carolina

Bac Si Reynolds had packed his old tiger stripe jacket. He slipped it on as he headed for the front desk to check out. A few of the ACEP physicians gave him a curious look.

Dave climbed into his Avis Mustang II convertible, and headed south. Once again his American Express card had passed electronic scrutiny.

The medical conference had been very informative and useful. It was good to see old residency mates from LAC/USC, but Dr. Reynolds was really looking forward to the SFA meeting. It had been almost thirty years, but sometimes it seemed like yesterday, since he had first stepped off the Pan American charter flight into the red dust and suffocating heat that was The Nam. He would never forget the body bags, stacked like cord wood at Tan Son Nut, nor the waiting pallets of brushed aluminum coffins.

Dave put down the top, and inhaled the lush North Carolina country side. His mind added the smell of cordite, burned and decaying human flesh, and spilled entrails. He shook the memory from his brain, and found 107.5 FM. "It wasn't me that started that crazy Asian war – but I was proud to go and do my patriotic chore, " came the voice of Kenny Rogers.

2130 EST, 4 August
room 814, Fayetteville Holiday Inn, N.C.

Wade Washington threw his suitcase on the bed and studied the room service menu. He didn't know if he wanted to go down to the dinning room tonight, or not. "Might as well go get a beer," he said to the empty room, as he slipped his S&W .38 chief's special under the pillow.

He pulled his battered green beret out of the Samsonite, and crunched it onto his balding, crewcut pate. Taking a moment to square the 5th Special Forces/Vietnam flash over his left eye. "De Oppresso Liber," read the scroll under the Randal fighting knife, and the crossed arrows.

"Fighting soldiers from the sky," Wade sang soto voice as he ambled down the hall, a slight swagger to his rotund bulk.

2345 EST, 4 August
Fayetteville Airport, North Carolina

The light beige and gold Citation settled on the tarmac, and taxied to the "General Aviation—Transient" area. Chad Tanner began the shut down checklist, as the ground crew approached.

"Feed and water her, give her a good rub down, then find her a dry stall," he told the ground crew chief, as he signed the necessary invoices.

The jet mechanic was used to all sorts of eccentricities from Lear and Citation owners, as well as from pilots in general. He didn't take much notice of the tall, tanned man wearing gray, python cowboy boots, WW II leather flight jacket, and olive-drab beret.

He had never seen the winged sword beret badge before.

"Who Dares Wins" read the script underneath.

2230 EST, 4 August
lounge, Holiday Inn, Fayetteville, N.C.

"Hey chief, haven't seen you in a coon's age," said a black face under an even blacker beret with a ragged hole directly over the scarred flesh that substituted for an eyebrow.

" Mister Chvostek to you Tipton," retorted Harry.

"Buy me a Jack Daniels, I've pulled the pin, effective next month."

"No shit! That's great! Hell! I'll buy you a case of fucking Jack Daniels!" answered Tipton.

The bar was rapidly filling with SF types, and the music was loud country western.

"Give us another round over here," commanded the three warriors in unison.

The pimply-faced bartender nodded in their direction. His father had wisely gone to Canada during the Vietnam conflict. Gonna be a long night, thought the kid as he squeezed lime into tequila.

Gonna be a great night, thought Harrison Q. Chvostek as he settled in the leatherette booth.

2200 est 4 August
lounge, Holiday Inn, Fayetteville

Mike Roberts sank into the booth with Harry Chvostek, Moses Tipton, and a man he did not recognize; but who was wearing a 5th Group flash on his beret.

"Thought I smelled something rank over in this corner. Hey gunny, you still pissin' on fires out in OR—E—GONE?"

"Little respect for a Battalion Chief, if you

please!" The bartender gave a dismayed glance at the new arrival. *Must be a better way to pay for college,* he thought.

2345 est 4 August
room 2313, Holiday Inn, Fayetteville

Judd Carmicheal studied the computer print-outs. Since he had not officially resigned, he still had unquestioned access to almost any file in the country.

He had cross-referenced with the SFA, the Holiday Inn reservations, the FBI, CIA, NCIC, as well as state and local law enforcement.

He found that all surviving members of LRRP TEAM COBRA would be at the reunion. He felt this would make a good place to start recruiting. "Probably all fat drunks by now," he said to himself.

Surprisingly, none had any serious felony convictions. John L. Murphy had two felonious assaults, and a disturbing the peace. The victim had apparently lived.

Murph must be getting soft, he thought as he poured two more fingers of Cuervo Gold.

Need someone better with a computer than I am, if we're going to keep the back door undetected. He scanned the roster again for a likely candidate.

He also wondered about Cecil Cedrick Tanner of Billings, Montana. He had listed his organization as SPECIAL AIR SERVICE, R.A.F., interesting!

1800 local 3 August
Quang Tri Province, DPRV

Nguen Lo watched the rain turning his fields into a sea of mud. The monkey was stewing in the pot with turnips, onions, hot Vietnamese chilies and a generous amount of nuc mam. He smiled at his children playing on the raised bamboo floor of the simple hut. Rain came in the cooking hole, spattering on the hot coals and cast iron.

The dampness bothered his ankles and knee. The knee had never properly healed after it shattered on the bulkhead of his flaming A6 Intruder. The ankles had both been smashed with the butt of an old .03 Springfield, after he had tried to escape from the reeducation camp. Both events were a lifetime ago.

He had all but forgotten Lt. J.G. Charles Everett Montgomery, USN.

He could not remember the faces of his parents, or even his EWO, who had not survived the bailout over the North Vietnamese canopy. He was Nguen Lo, loyal citizen of the DEMOCRATIC PEOPLES REPUBLIC OF VIETNAM. He gave his wife a kiss and a pat on her gently swollen abdomen. *I should have a son before harvest,* he thought.

He found a place at the communal pot. Incense was burning at the base of the smiling Budda. The family nodded their heads respectfully in his direction, in thanks for the meal.

Chapter Five

0800 EST 5 AUGUST
room 814

The harsh ring of the phone woke John Murphy, *too damn early,* he thought. The night before had run too long. He groped for the annoying instrument, intending to unhook the receiver when he found it. Something told him to put it to his ear, "Murphy, you there?" "Uhhh," Murphy managed, his head was swimming in a purple fog, and he tried to focus on the LED of the bedside clock. "This is BUCKSHOT, MEET ME FOR BREAKFAST, DINING ROOM, 0830," commanded the anonymous voice. Before he could answer, John was listening to the dial tone.

A flood of memories snapped SGT/MAJOR John L. Murphy, U.S. Army Special Forces, (Airborne) [Ret.] to wakefulness. BUCKSHOT was Cobra Team's operational code name in the MAC-V/SOG CCN days. The last time he had heard that word had been a very bad day in the Nam.

What the Fuck! I'm a Goddamn truck driver, for Christ's sake, I don't play this bull-shit anymore. The long, angry scar running from just under his left jaw to his right nipple was aching. His heart was pounding in his chest like a pile-driver.

0800 EST, 5 August
room 187

Dr. Dave Reynolds splashed cold water in his face. *I haven't gotten that shit faced since residency, never again,* he thought remorsefully. BUCKSHOT had called him three minutes after the call to room 814.

This is impossible. Probably a team member's sick attempt at humor, he thought. But he knew he had to respond. Old habits were hard to break.

0830 EST, 5 August
Dinning Room

Battalion Chief Mike Roberts, CFD, had only served with the joint operations Cobra Team for nine months, but Buckshot compelled him to meet whoever the hell had called. He scanned the handful of morning diners. The previous night had run long for most of the conventioneers. A vaguely familiar silhouette was hunched over his cup in a far corner, by an open window. He was secluded from the other breakfasters.

Older, grayer, thinner, but it was the former C.O. of the elite LRRP team, thought Mike as he approached tentatively. *Is this his idea of a joke?* wondered Mike. Mike had not remembered a particularly humorous side to the colonel.

0828 EST, 5 August
third floor, Holiday Inn

Wade Washington had abruptly left the supple, young Nubian he had brought home late last night. She was leaning out the door; rewarding the early morning risers with an unabashed view of her generous, firm, bare bosom. "Asshole!" she shouted to Wade's retreating back.

0831 EST, 5 August
Dinning room

Greetings were mumbled, as the five surviving team members of the "Brightlight" team drew around the isolated breakfast table.

When the men had settled and ordered coffee, Judd began without preamble, "I know you all have lives of your own, and I don't have the right to ask."

The aging warriors knew he did have the right to ask anything. He had earned that right, as well as the DSC, when he brought his team out of Laos, passing through an NVA company strength unit.

"From this point on everything is classified. A 'Need to know, Eyes only' basis. You can leave anytime you feel uncomfortable. We have a mission," said Judd.

He paused to let that sink in, and register.

"The mission is NOT, I repeat, NOT officially sanctioned. Our chances of survival are slim to none."

The waitress brought coffee and was advised that no one would be eating. She dismissed the table.

The team, for they had once again began thinking of themselves as a team, knew she would not be back.

Judd used his finely honed peripheral vision to check, without appearing to check, to see if the other diners had taken any note of their conversation. All were engrossed in eggs and hash-browns. However, a sallow-faced, dour man, wearing a checked Pendleton shirt did glance briefly in the team's general direction.

He continued, sotto voiced, "We all know the U.S. abandoned our guys in Vietnam. I want to go get them."

The coffee sat ignored, as the men at the table tried to digest the colonel's statement. They all knew of his DIA status.

This is crazy. I've got a wife, kids, job, family, bills, it's been years since I've been shot at. ABSOLUTELY FUCKING CRAZY! ,was the combined thought of three of the candidates.

Wade Washington thought, *Why not?*

No one wanted to speak first, as Judd studied his team.

Do these guys still have it? He wasn't sure, but did not know where else to look, nor who to ask.

He did know that he would rather go into combat with these men, than any others he had ever met.

"You should also know, that effective one September, I am no longer a member of the intelligence community. Nor am I, in any manner whatsoever, affiliated with the government of the United States.

1200 EST, 6 August
room 2313

Chad Tanner sipped his tea, and tried to decide if the leathery yank sitting across from him was completely out of his bloody mind.

"I have access to certain U.S. government and United Kingdom files and records. Be assured that I know you infinitely better than you know me. I fee you would be a valuable addition to a proposed venture I have in mind.

However, it needs to be thoroughly understood, this mission is not sanctioned under the auspices of the government of either country. Nor am I a representative of either government," explained Judd.

1135 EST, 6 August
Oval Office, D.C.

President Caldwell finished reading the POW/MIA report completed by the CIA/DIA. It had taken twenty seven, single spaced, typed pages to reiterate the official position, and to prove the nonexistence of live Americans in Southeast Asia. *How the hell do you prove nonexistence?* the CIC wondered.

He had not heard directly from Judd Carmicheal. Richard Markam had told him of J.D.'s overnight mail resignation postmarked: Fayetteville, North Carolina.

0600 local, 6 August
Vigilant Leader, labor/reeducation camp, DPRV

Tran watched his "cattle" working the flooded rice paddies, as the sun rose abruptly from behind the low lying mountains of his country's northernmost province.

Just beyond those hills lay the sleeping dragon, Vietnam's traditional enemy, the Peoples Republic of China.

Tran worried that the collapse of the protective umbrella, the Union of Soviet Socialist Republics, would bring the dragon across the mountains.

He adjusted the sling on his AKM and turned his attention to the laboring "war criminals". They had been captured, tried, and convicted long before Tran joined the People's Revolutionary Guard. He was sure one of them had dropped the CBU that had destroyed his village, and killed his family.

It was good to see them broken and bent, mindlessly toiling to rebuild a strong united Annam.

The sun beat relentlessly on the bowed, leathery backs of the Caucasians. Some were harnessed like draft water buffaloes. Others were caring for the tender shoots.

The prisoners did not even look up, or notice the squadron of Hind 24s as they swooped low overhead. None could remember the days when they too soared among the clouds. The PK machine gun in the ominous tower was superfluous. Tran had not even heard of an escape attempt in his lifetime. These eagles had truly crashed and burned.

2330 EST, 8 August
Crandal, Michigan

Christine Murphy settled in John's Barco recliner, dad's chair. She had surprised him with it for their fourteenth wedding anniversary. She reread his cryptic letter.

The bottle of Leelanau Chablis was almost empty, as she filled the fluted glass. *Is this some kind of perverted mid-life crisis? Does he have a girlfriend? What the HELL is going on?* she thought.

"Try to understand," the prose pleaded, "I'll be home when I get home. There's something I have to do, and I have to do it now. Kiss the kids Babe. You have to believe I love you. Please believe that, take care Babe."

She had tried to call Fayetteville, but John had checked out earlier that day. His letter said he'd, 'be in touch when I can'.

The last time she'd had this wrenching in her gut, and ominous sense of foreboding, was when she'd watched him walk out the door, duffel bag over his shoulder, on his last "Delta" alert. That had turned out to be the fiasco, code named "rice bowl", at "Desert One".

He had come home from that one with 34% TBS burns, but he had survived, he always did.

Christine had endured, and endeavored to be a good special operations wife. This was possibly harder than being a good special operations troop. She had hung in there, not knowing, not wanting to know. *But goddamn it, that's all over, or was it?*

Princess, their calico cat, climbed on her lap and settled in. Only one of them would find sleep tonight.

Christine poured another glass of Chablis and pressed her damp face into the cat's fur.

2130 EST, 8 August
Georgetown, Virginia

The door chimes startled Cindy Carmicheal. She was more startled to see the tall, gaunt figure standing in the rain, hat in hand.

"Mr. Markam, come in, you're getting soaked." He stepped into the foyer. He apologized to Cindy, as a puddle formed on Judd Carmicheal's terrazzo, "Excuse the hour, but I just got this, and, ahh, thought you might have some insight." He was holding a Federal Express Overnight Letter envelope in his hand.

He had already informed the President, and the security council. Steps were being taken to change J.D. Carmicheal's status in the intelligence community, even as he spoke.

Cindy knew what the distinctive red, white and blue envelope contained.

Damn his soul. He had promised to wait until

after the convention. After they had discussed it. What the hell happens to the male of the species when they approach fifty? Male menopause? Mid-life crisis? Juvenile delinquency? What? Next he'd find himself some nineteen year old air head who'd be impressed with his heroic, macho bullshit! Maybe he already has, thought Cindy.

Over the cappuccino she read her husband's formal, official, polite letter of resignation:

Insurmountable personal differences, professional growth, individual moral and ethical dilemma, a privilege and honor to have served, etc. No details, no reason. Effective upon receipt.

She didn't know why she was defending her husband. But she did know her husband did not like nor trust the man sitting across from her, with his pinky properly extended, sipping his drink. There was a frothy brown crust to his sparse gray mustache, as he settled the cup and spoke in a reassuring, politician's voice, "I want you to know that I am not going to accept Judd's resignation at this point in time. I have given him an indefinite leave of absence to get his head together." *And for my people to find him,* he thought to himself.

"He has sufficient time-in-grade on active federal status to draw full pay for six to eight months. If he has not changed his mind in that time he is certainly eligible for full retirement. Please talk this over with Judd and have him contact me. He has my private number, day or night."

Right, if he even stays in touch with me, she thought dejectedly. But what she said was, "Certainly Mr. Markam, as soon as he returns from Fayetteville I'll have him call you. He just needs some time."

0800 EST, 9 August
Brigham Young University, Utah

Sheila Cannon had not known her older brother. He had taken a SAM over Haiphong Harbor during Operation Rolling Thunder, while she was still working on toilet training.

Sheila had spent her life studying the Vietnam Conflict/War. She had stacks of photos, old 8mm movies, T.V. news footage, recently declassified documents, and everything the Freedom of Information Act could afford her.

She kept a faded black and white eight by ten glossy, now sealed in nineties acrylic, on her dorm desk. It depicted a handsome, athletic, Viking standing proudly, one hand resting on his F4 warbird.

His body had never been recovered. "–regret to inform you–missing in action presumed to be dead–deepest sympathies."

He had been officially declared KIA in 1975.

She finished stuffing envelopes for the American League of Families, as she watched the latest DIA/CIA study decrying the possibility of live American POWs. This study was in response to Yeltsin's pronouncement. The news broadcast was interposed with all too familiar, and still painful, combat clips from the sixties and seventies. It closed with protest coverage, to make it well rounded and catholic in it's coverage. A lone tear tracked down the poly-sci' major's face.

0830 local, 9 August
over Boise, Idaho

Mike Roberts sipped his Absolut bloody Mary, and tried to organize his thoughts. Surprisingly, the aisle and center seats of the 747 were empty. The attractive, young brunette flight attendant had left him a fresh drink. His mind churned as he watched her firm tight ass roll seductively down the narrow passageway.

He tried to piece together the all night sessions the team had held in room 2313.

The pictures, letters, computer print-outs, classified and unclassified documents, all blurred into a dizzying dialog.

All the men from MACV-SOG had been "Q" ("ultra") cleared a quarter of a century ago, and once they'd been good. Probably some of the best. *But now? Had Judd Carmicheal finally fallen off that precarious edge he'd been living on for so long?*

I'm not going to do it! This is absolutely fuckin'-A insane, to hell with it and to hell with them! But Mike knew he had to do it or die trying.

Ah, she's coming back. She looks pretty good from the front too. I'd like to bury my face in those bazookas. 'Tits like a forty dollar milk cow', as my pop used to say. Mike fingered his black hills gold wedding ring, rubbing his thumb across the knurled leaves. *See you are going insane. Think you're nineteen again? Never again old buddy. Must be Alzheimer's or male menopause. Whatever it is, it'll probably kill me,* he thought.

0900 MST, 10 August
El Paso, Texas

"You just came back, and now you want an indefinite leave of absence? I've got a hospital to run. I can't kiss every doctor's ass. Do you think you're special because you're some kind of war hero? Check the dates on your clippings doctor, that's ancient fucking history. You're medals are rusty for Christ's sake."

Dave was worried the florid faced administrator would suffer a Myocardial Infarction, or embolic event in front of his eyes. The over weight, out of shape, chain smoker's neck veins were distended, his eyes were bulging, and his face was bright crimson.

"Sir, my contract states, ah–." Dr. Reynolds paused as the hospital director was almost apoplectic. Drool trickled down the corner of his cyanotic lips as he stammered.

"Out, get the hell out! Come back when you want, or better yet, not at all."

Dr. Dave Reynolds backed out of the enraged bureaucrat's office. He was now even more sure this had to be the craziest thing he had ever even contemplated. He still did not know what to tell Lila.

He took the stairs and left through the laundry area, afraid he'd run into his lover of three years before he had the proper lie formulated.

They were going to spend the weekend up at Ruidosso. *Maybe that's a good time. Is there ever a good time?* he wondered.

1200 PST, 9 August
Columbia, Oregon

"Mike you do not hunt. You can't stroll in here and announce you're going somewhere in God knows where, Montana, and start packing. Jesus Christ on a crutch, you just got home. I swear, every time you get with your Nam buddies you get a little bit crazier, but you've always snapped back before you went completely off the deep end."

She bit her lip and changed gears, desperate to save her man, her life, not sure where they were both headed.

"Honey, I love you. Talk to me. What is going on? What about the Fire Department? Do you just need some time? Just tell me, and I can deal with it."

Mike felt like the biggest shit since Adam gave Eve the clap. He knew he had to go and he knew he could not tell his wife why or where. "Honey, I want to go hunting with some guys in Montana. I've got lots of comp' time coming at the department. You and the kids will be fine. I have to go. Just give me some time, I'll write," he asked.

She knew he wouldn't. He was digging in his old foot locker for his web gear.

2329 EST, 9 August
Langley, Virginia

Thomas Darrow had been Hiram Caldwell's friend and confidant over forty years. They had met during their freshman year at Francis Xavier High, when both had been vying for a track scholarship, and the same blond cheerleader. Neither had gotten the scholarship nor the blond. Last Tom had heard, she was a fat happy grandmother, married to a Certified Public Accountant in Hackensack, New Jersey.

Darrow and Caldwell had fought their way through Annapolis, then through Basic Infantry Officer's Training on "the island".

Both men had been shavetail second lieutenants leading platoons into the Republic of Korea. They had emerged from the "Frozen Chozon" as "old men" in charge of what was left of two companies of the 3rd Marine Division.

Thomas S. Darrow, USMC, now wore the simple blue and white enameled ribbon of the Navy Cross on his lapel. He had earned "The Cross" and a captaincy due to a "close encounter of the lethal kind", with a Russian T34 tank.

Over the years Thomas Darrow had served as campaign manager, assistant to congressman Caldwell, then cabinet advisor to the Vice-President, and now National Security Advisor to President Hiram Caldwell.

This was the President's second term. The constitution prohibited a third. Time for both men to retire to the good life. But first, one last chore.

Tom was using his personal computer to access CIA files of known arms dealers, always of a somewhat nefarious nature, to meet his friend's latest request.

He sure hoped the PUS knew what he was doing, *but ours is not to reason why, etc., Semper Fi!*

He had also covertly established funding for J.D. Carmicheal's improbable mission through a circumflex maize of blind pouches and arbitrage. *The mission was going to have enough obstacles without money being one of them.*

He had also established fifty thousand dollar life insurance policies for each of the team members of "Operation Bougainvillea". This was set up via a series of discreet deposits with the very discreet Swiss banking community. *At least we can take care of these guys' families. It's not the families fault their breadwinners' decided to play cowboy one last time.* He very much doubted any of the on-ground players would survive.

He was due to have another clandestine meeting with Carmicheal on August tenth. *That crazy mother might just pull it off,* he thought.

His marching orders from the President were in effect—leave no stone unturned, but don't make a ripple.

Well at least he wasn't an ass-in-the-grass grunt anymore, this was bad enough.

Ah, here's a likely character. I should be able to get all manner of explosive toys from this guy, if the price is right. It would be.

0800 EST, 10 August
Langley, Virginia

Judd couldn't remember when he'd slept more than a few hours at a stretch since his steam room meeting with his CIC. But the team and the plan were taking shape.

He reread the blue-gray screen of his lap top P.C. It's limited memory augmented by a modem connecting him via the President's "back door", with a room full of computers in Washington, D.C.

He had settled on "Bougainvillea" as an operational code name. Bougainvillea was a serendipitous vine with sharp thorns and beautiful, fragrant, magenta flowers, that entwined, uncultivated, across most of Southeast Asia.

He had adhered closely to Clausewitz; recalled by the pneumonic, MMMOUSSSE. He knew from his days at "The Point" that any commander who ignored the Prussian general's principles was doomed to the proverbial "shit storm".

He called them upon his screen, and reviewed each one:

Mission
Mass

Maneuver
Unity of command
Security
Surprise
Economy of force

Judd had added a third "S" for Speed. Lack of speed kills, particularly in small unit, commando style missions.

The centuries old formulae always worked if it was properly applied, and if you had good troops and a good portion of luck.

John reviewed his team roster like a mantra: John L. Murphy, Michael (NMN) Roberts, Harrison D. Chvostek, Cecil Cedrick Tanner, III, Wade Carver Washington, Dr. David Aloysious Reynolds, and Moses Tipton.

Aging warriors, himself included, determined to bring their friends home. *Hang in there amigos,* he thought.

All night secessions in Fayetteville, fueled by a paper blizzard, tons of coffee, and a fair amount of ethanol had convinced these otherwise sane, sensible, responsible, adult, private citizens to venture once more into the "valley of the shadow of death." *For we are the meanest sons-a-bitches in the valley!*

The President's envoy was due any moment. Harrison Chvostek had taken lump sum leave settlement, and "ROADed" (Retired On Active Duty), and was ensconced with his computers at a remote site in Montana.

Chapter Six

0700 MST, 10 August
"Star Corral", "Rocking 'T'" ranch, Montana

Mule deer grazed fearlessly around the old barracks at the base of the box canyon. The place where hundreds of Japanese-Americans had been "relocated" from the west coast in the opening days of WW II. A brook, teaming with rainbow and cutthroat trout, meandered through the acreage.

Chad Tanner had refurbished one of the larger buildings into a close approximation of a Welsh country lodge. This was his favorite "get away"; especially when Terry was in residence at the main house.

His children had lined the walls with stuffed animal heads, deer, elk, moose, antelope, bear, and various small game and fowl. They had also crowded the mantel with the plastic, gold plated statues, much sought after in school sports. Pennants and winning game balls completed the atmosphere. The collection was interposed with Chad's military awards, certificates, and memorabilia. All in all, a good place to sit by a roaring fire, hoist a pint, and remember and reflect. Terry hated the place and only visited it once, at the end of construction.

It seemed totally incongruous that seven warriors now sat in this quiet, peaceful, special place planning a deadly, covert mission.

Chvostek had a large map of the DPRV spread over the patina of the hand polished hard wood floor. Stacks of photos, documents, and computer print-outs littered the large high-beamed, open room. Red felt tip circles bled across the map. Each one identifying live sightings, and probable holding areas. He still found it hard to believe the government he, and all the men left behind in Vietnam, had served so honorably, trusted so completely, the country they loved more than life, knew all this information, and had gone to such an effort to suppress, bury, and cover it up.

HumInt and ElInt sources indicated two likely sights: VIGILANT LEADER REEDUCATION CAMP & PHU DUC PRISON.

They were both on the DPRV/PRC border about twenty kilometers from each other. Obviously Team Bougainvillea couldn't hit both locations. Colonel Carmicheal would have to pick one. When a primary target had been assigned, a full scale mockup would be constructed, and the rescue rehearsed, honed and finely tuned. Let the games begin.

Stacks of armaments, ordinance and building materials had already arrived. Fortunately the Montana State Police were critically under funded and undermanned.

The county sheriff's office had neither the resources nor the interest in trespassing on the sprawling acreage of one of the state's biggest taxpayers. Harry was sure the A.T.F. would have been very interested in the goings on at the "Rocking 'T'".

Chief Chvostek's duty with SEAL Team Six had

taught him not to question the origin of intelligence nor supplies if he had no "need to know".

0700 MST, 10 August
"Star Corral"

It was still cool at seven thousand two hundred feet above sea level and the sun had not yet risen over the canyon rim. The men of Team Bougainvillea had already sweated through T-shirts and gym trunks, as Moses Tipton lead them through their morning P.T. They knew "lean and mean fighting machine" was an obtainable goal. They'd all been there once; but they'd all forgotten how much it hurt.

What hurt even more, was the knowledge that the grueling calisthenics would be followed by a two mile run.

"We'll start with two miles," promised the athletic, black, former SEAL who had not, and of course never would, let himself go to pot.

MREs, Meals Ready to Eat, which were neither, were stacked in readiness for the after run repast. Judd had decided the quickest way to get his team ready for the mission was to immerse them in military genre'. The sweating men had to admit it felt good, damn good!

Liquor had also been banned for the duration. Judd had promised one hell of a bash after the mission. It was a promise he sincerely looked forward to fulfilling.

A big "muley" and his doe watched the cavorting humans curiously from the thick foliage of the hillside.

1022 local, 11 August

GRU HQ., Moscow, UER

Captain Second Rank Mikhail Gorky looked down onto the park named after his famous great uncle, a "Hero of the Soviet Union", and tried to decide if he was, in fact, an enemy of the state, and traitor to Rodina.

He had been ordered to purge an entire bank of computer records in the wake of Yeltsin's public pronouncement of live American POWs.

Mikhail had been a low level agent for the capitalist pigs, most of his career in the soviet military. He had passed just enough information to afford his dacha and transient mistresses over the years.

He had even slipped in a extra tidbit now and again to get small gifts for his fat, stupid cow of a wife and her screaming brood.

Captain Second Rank Gorky felt loyal to the motherland, and had never given the Americans any information that would really harm her. It had usually been low-tech. information which he felt they already had anyway.

Certainly the most recently transmitted information only involved Russia's little primate brothers, who were still swinging from Asian trees.

He had left the bulky manila envelope, full of computer print-outs and photos, at the prearranged location in Gorky park. He was still awaiting his compensation. He knew it would be very generous.

The prisoner roster alone, dated this very year, would be worth a wheelbarrow full of rubles. Of course nowadays, it took a wheel barrow full of rubles to buy a decent vodka.

Mikhail also was not sure what was to become of the Military Intelligence Directorate, and thus to him, in the Unified Eurasian Republics. *Maybe a change of scenery was in order, surely the Americans would help now.*

0930 EST, 10 August
Langely, Virginia

Judd opened the motel door to the length of the chain, with his left hand; his Walther PPK was behind his back in his right hand.

"Buckshot?" asked the tall, well groomed gentleman in the Brooks Brother's three-piece, and the Harvard old school tie.

Judd released the chain and shook the NSA's hand. Contrary to his usual wariness; Judd liked the aging politician instantly. *Hand seems callused for a bureaucrat?* he thought.

Thomas Darrow noted the stacks of print-outs, photos and yellow legal pads. He could not make out the scribbling that was covering the pads, including the margins.

"The President conveys his well wishes, Mr. Carmicheal," he said as he handed Judd a typed list of the arrangements that were already in place. He glanced at his Rolex Oyster, saying, "by now some of the material' and supplies should have arrived at your staging area. More are on the way."

He continued, "If you approve of this individual, I will give him the appropriate coordinates, and he will proceed at all due speed to that location." The National Security Advisor handed Judd a "201" file.

Judd opened the file at the black and white photo of a full-blooded Sioux, dressed in a tiger stripe flight suit and standing in front of a Cobra gunship. He read Frank Romero Morningstar's record.

Most of his service had been with Air America, the CIA and MACV-SOG. He carried a "Q" clearance, and had been involved with black operations his entire career. Morningstar was qualified on practically everything that flew, short of a 747, and was currently listed as unemployed.

Apparently there had been a rather violent disagreement with the Director of Central Intelligence. Judd liked that.

"He'll do," was all Carmicheal said as he closed the file and placed it on his growing stack.

"This may also be of some interest. It arrived via COMSAT just this morning. I was able to, ah, intercept it. The Agency does not, repeat, does not have this information, nor shall they." He handed Judd a manila envelope.

Inside were photos of gaunt Caucasians, dejectedly circling a dusty compound. The enclosed roster was dated this year. The location was Phu Duc Prison. The roster listed seventeen American war criminals. Judd made his primary target decision.

"Have these names been cross referenced with DOD files?" Judd asked hoarsely.

"Affirmative," came the soft reply.

"We have to push the clock forward," Judd said.

He was pacing the room like a caged panther. "Hell, with this confirmation Caldwell can send in the Fucking Marines for Christ's sake!" J.D. exclaimed.

"With the collapse of the iron curtain, destruction of the Berlin Wall, and cooling of the cold war, ah, certain political and diplomatic negotiations prohibit that particular course of action at this particular point in time. Overt action would not be politically expedient.

Besides, do you really think the gooks would let those POWs live once we sat foot on the sovereign soil of the Democratic People's Republic of Vietnam?" the NSA answered calmly.

More politician doublespeak, thought J.D.

Judd handed him two lists of equipment and material'.

"One is stuff I'll need at the staging area. One is the equipment I need delivered in-country. Can you arrange it?" he asked.

The President's envoy scanned the two, double-spaced, typewritten lists.

"Seems reasonable," he replied. He then carefully creased the pages precisely down the center and placed them in the inside pocket of his charcoal pinstripe.

1130 MST, 12 August
"Star Corral"

As the unmarked, dull black C-130 descended through the cloudless Montana sky it was tracked by three SMAWs. The commandos were expecting a plane and pilot, but they were not at all sure this was it.

When the Flying Boxcar had settled at the end of the dusty tarmac, normally used by Chad Tanner's Citation, three sets of crosshairs of the man portable Shoulder Mounted Multipurpose Assault Weapons settled on the body of the ungainly aircraft. Three index fingers curled on cold steel triggers.

An unmarked, khaki colored HUMV bearing four unsmiling troopers, clad in SADF camo BDUs sans insignia, materialized out of the dust cloud the C-130's four turboprops had stirred up. They were all armed with CAR 15s, locked and loaded, set on full auto.

The ramp of the big cargo plane slowly opened like the gaping maw of some prehistoric beast. The short, solidly built native of the Black Hills ambled into the Montana sunlight and the muzzles of the assault weapons.

"This must be Camp Bougainvillea?" he drawled. He had the burnished tone and noble bearing America had earnestly tried to extinguish.

Safeties clicked on and rifles lowered as Judd Carmicheal advanced and extended an unarmed hand.

"I've got ordinance on board if I can get a hand unloading," said Frank Morningstar.

Weapons were slung as the team bent to the task; live fire practice would begin tomorrow.

The rough mockup of Phu Duc prison had been erected the previous night.

After the equipment had been stored, the team relaxed with cold cokes and introduced themselves. They had all chewed the same dirt.

Judd used computer graphics and an old fashioned sand mock up to lay out the plan, and Area of Operations.

It was explained to Frank that he and his aircraft would play a pivotal role. It was also explained that Chad Tanner would be his back-up pilot in the very likely event he was killed.

The group would do a HAHO insertion from the 130 and hopefully the extraction also.

"We'll come in over the PRC and jump at twenty eight thousand. We will be wearing OBAs, (Oxygen Breathing Apparatus), using para-foils. We'll deploy at a thousand feet and cross into gookville. We should be on terra firma in this group of hills ten to fifteen klicks north of the prison," Judd explained as it were a done deal already.

The team wished they felt as confident, so did Judd.

Their commander continued, "There is an air strip approximately eight kilometers to the southwest, Freedom Bird will pick us up there. Should be quick, clean and surgical. We've all done it before."

Yeah, back when Christ was a corporal, thought Wade Washington.

"What about the other place, uh, Watchful Leader or whatever?" asked Reynolds.

"We'll have to leave that mission to the State Department. If we pull this one off and bring some live POWs home, it'll push their hand and they'll have to demand a full accounting," Judd answered.

Real time SURSAT photos of the A.O. ringed the map. No one questioned their authenticity.

0300 MST, 13 August
"Star Corral"

There are three kinds of night in Montana, pitch black, flood of full moon, and the eerie glow that comes from a big sky shot full of stars. This was one of the latter. A thumbnail of moon hid modestly in a corner, not even trying to compete with the thousands of brightly glowing jewels.

It was so bright, the Night Vision Devices were not really needed. They took the crisp clear ambient light and enhanced it to the point that

Phu Duc Prison looked like Dodge City at High Noon. *An apt allusion,* thought Moses Tipton. He remembered the ghostly green seen through the NVDs under the lush triple canopy of the Laotian jungle.

He tread softly, giving hand signals to the rest of the team. They had configured the mockup for the contingency of antipersonnel mines and trip-flares. The guard towers were manned with one hundred pound sand bags.

Informed sources indicated that the real ones would have KPV 14.5mm heavy machine guns in two of the four towers, with AK-74s in the other two. They were arranged to provide a withering cross-fire.

The tiger cages were arranged in a horse shoe around the exercise yard. Each cage also held a one hundred pound sand bag. Dr. Reynolds had predicted that to be the approximate weight of the captured Americans, judging from the photos and presumed diet and living conditions. Seventeen sand bags, equaled seventeen lives.

Swift, silent, deadly. Improvise, adapt, overcome! thought Mike Roberts, as he put a hard wood quarrel from his crossbow into each guard tower sand bag.

So far, so good. At least it wasn't this cold in the Nam, thought Tipton as he back crawled through the concertina wire. He thought he had tripped some kind of electronic warning system until he realized it was a damn coyote, *spooky fucker.*

The crisp, starlit night exploded with the distinctive pop of a 5.45mm on full auto. The green tracers fluoresced in the air, and the dancing shadows produced by parachute flares lit the compound. The team scrambled for cover as the dusty geysers erupted around them. Judd Carmicheal strode into the center of the eerily illuminated exercise yard, the smoking AK at port arms. "Gentlemen, let's run through it again," he ordered.

Chapter Seven

13 August to 15 September
"Star Corral" staging area, Montana

Team Bougainvillea was becoming a lean, mean, fighting machine; more importantly, they were becoming a finely honed team . They were ready, willing and able to perform the mission. They knew that everyday of their preparation was a day closer to the end of despair for the untold numbers of comrades in arms, languishing in the prisons of Southeast Asia. They could not begin to fathom the mental condition of the prisoners after twenty-plus years of captivity. They tried not to dwell on that particular aspect of the mission.

Would there be anything worth bringing home? Would they even know where home was? Better not to think too much about it, they thought collectively.

Chad's wife was in Europe on an extended, international shopping tour.

Frank Morningstar only heard from his sundry ex-wives when he missed a child support or alimony payment.

John Murphy had gotten a letter at the Billings' P.O. box they all used: "I still don't know what you are doing or why, but I do know that it's important or you wouldn't be doing it. And I do know that I love you and I am afraid for you. Write when you can, I'll be waiting," she had written.

Mike Roberts had received a similar letter.

Harry Chvostek had cabled his father to get the Maui operations off the ground.

Dave Reynolds had not written to Lila, nor to the hospital administrator.

Wade Washington had no one to write to.

Moses Tipton had sent post cards to his more favorite lady loves.

Judd Carmicheal had not written since his letter to Markam.

The run-throughs were getting tougher and tougher, thanks to Chvostek's computer skills. He had rigged chained DShK machine guns, trip flares, antipersonnel mines and motion detectors to the mockup of the prison. Depending on his mood, and how creative he was feeling on a particular evening, he would program all or some of the electronic countermeasures to deploy.

He had loaded the claymores and Bouncing Betty antipersonnel devices with a disgusting shade of yellow-green acrylic paint. The victim looked as if he had been bombed with baby shit.

The machine guns and Squad Automatic Weapons were firing blank ammunition, but every tenth round was a tracer. The red hot, glowing projectile was a painful reminder to keep your head and your ass down.

Their HAHO jump took them over the Northeast corner of Yellowstone National Park. The soaring descent over the vast Montana/Wyoming countryside was awe inspiring. Chvostek's computer had prepared an ambush at the Drop Zone just to keep every one on their toes.

Morning P.T., the run was now up to six miles,

was followed by debriefing and equipment checks. The afternoon and early evening were given to rest and reflection. The nights were spent rehearsing the mission.

Blisters, sun burn, sprained ankles, muscle aches and pains were mostly ignored, as was the steady diet of the tasteless MREs.

Judd Carmicheal went over the mission and studied the latest AGI and COMSAT information as he sipped his coffee. *The team was ready.*

0400 local, 1 September
Moscow, UER

The more things change, the more they stay the same. Two black, official Zils were parked in front of the dreary, gray, apartment building.

A firm knock awoke Captain Second Rank Mikhail Gorky and his spouse. There had been an irregularity noted at the GRU and Gorky's presence was requested at once. He would be escorted to the GHQ of the ARKR, soviet command and control, which still managed to exist in the UER.

Certain documents that would embarrass the state had been compromised. The dour faced police colonel thought Captain Gorky may have some insight into the situation.

Mikhail's heart sank. He knew he would never see America. He was surprised to find that he would even miss his wife and children.

0400 local, 1 September
Bangkok, Thailand

Sergi' Mahoney was the son of a Russian mother, and Irish-Catholic father. He envisioned himself a citizen of the world. He had been a gunrunner, now called an arms dealer, for the highest bidder ever since his service with the Legion Estrange.

He had left most of his left arm, and his left eye at Dien Bien Phu.

He did not know why his old acquaintance had placed this particular order for the toys of war; but it was premium dollar and thus bought his total loyalty for this single transaction. He also personally approved of the likely target. He had long since discounted the Vietnamese as a non-human species.

Sergi' strolled through the warehouse and ticked off the items on his list. Heavy bribes and counter-bribes had been paid. The buyer seemed not to mind. *Must be a small unit assault:*

1 fully equipped BTR-50 armored vehicle w/ AK-630, 12 electronic remote detonators, 2 cases C4 plastique' explosive, 3 hand held satellite transmitters w/ burst capability, 6 Charge-coupled devices, 1 case Fog Forming Foam grenades, 1 case smoke grenades, 1 case M3 antipersonnel grenades, 3 hundred foot coils gold line climbing rope, 1 man portable InfraRed Imaging Unit, 1 man portable RPO flame weapon, 1 case 5.56mm full metal jacketed ammunition, 1 case 9mm semi-jacketed, hollow point pistol ammo.

Must be bringing in their own small arms, thought Sergi' as he double checked to make sure all numbers and identification markings had been sufficiently obliterated.

He had been well compensated for the extra effort, to deliver the cache to the assigned map coordinates just across the border from the Peoples Republic of China.

Just into goddamn Indochina, he thought bitterly.

2300 MST, 4 September
"Star Corral"

Judd gathered his team in the cozy den. He had received a cryptic telex, *All in place. Lock and load. Good luck.* It had been unsigned.

It had been decided they would make the HAHO jump lightly armed and equipped. Picking up needed armament from an in-country location. They would jump sterile. All were dressed in South African Defense Force camouflaged Battle Dress Uniforms. All labels and insignia had been removed. Rings, watches, necklaces, and identification were locked in Chad Tanner's wall safe. Chronosport UDT wrist chronometers had been issued and synchronized to Greenwich Mean Time. All had ALICE load bearing web gear with multiple pouches. All had attached a 91C, basic field medic kit. They did not know how many casualties would occur among the team, nor the true condition of the POWs.

Each team member carried a Baretta M-9, semiautomatic pistol in a low slung SWAT thigh holster.

Each commando had taped a razor sharp KBAR fighting knife to his shoulder harness, upside down for quick access. M-16s and CAR-15s completed the armament. The rest they would find waiting for them in Vietnam, *at least they sincerely hoped they would.*

All serial numbers had been filed. Camouflage face paint and crushed boonie hats topped off the costume.

The rehearsals and training were over. This was the mission. Mouths were dry, pulses were slightly elevated. *It seemed cold for September.*

The team would board the C-130 at first light

five September and fly due west for over twenty four hours. They would lose a day crossing the international date line.

Somehow, air-to-air refueling had been arranged without arousing too much suspicion. The U.S. Air Force was used to following orders without question, provided they came with sufficient authority. These had come from the National Security Advisor personally.

The CIA and especially the DIA were sniffing around as if they smelled a bitch in heat, but as yet had not uncovered the mission.

The next time these men set foot on solid ground, they would, once again be in hostile country without their country's official sanction or approval. *So what else is new?*

Most sat in various degrees of half sleep, and waited for the glow of dawn. The time for discussion and conversation had long since passed.

Chad and Frank went over the flight plan for the umpteenth time, comparing it with the latest satellite weather predictions. They could use the auto-pilot and avionics as long as the atmospherics cooperated.

0700 local, 4 September
Quang Tri Province, DPRV

Nguen Lo patched his bamboo thatch roof against the assault of the monsoon rains. The village political officer had been replaced by a younger, more fanatical official directly from Hanoi.

He knew he should start preparing for the arrival of his new son, the entire village would share in the celebration. He knew it would not be so long now. The cold and the rain made his knee ache.

0700 local, 4 September
Phu Duc Prison, DPRV

Lt. Colonel James D. Bogart, USAF shuffled around the exercise yard. He was stooped from the years, and old compression fractures in his spine. The bailout door in the nose of his B-52 had malfunctioned. The ejection seat had slammed downward into the still partially closed steel hatch. He had learned to live with the pain; it was actually minor compared with the pain of his unending captivity.

He had long ago learned not to talk to his yard companions. He could not remember exactly when he had given up all hope of escape or rescue or release, but it had been long ago. His only escape would be when his heart finally stopped it's relentless beating. Until that time he placed one foot in front of the other, on his preordained journey.

Captain Matthew Cannon, USAF followed second in line behind Colonel Bogart. Over the years a lockstep formation had developed. Day after day, month after month, year after year the same monotonous parade like a dripping faucet.

His childhood LDS beliefs kept his faith in the after-life. There was also a faint glimmer of hope that flickered periodically in an inexplicable fashion. *The rain feels good, it reminds you that you are still alive.*

Lieutenant Commander Joshua Bourke, USN limping on the stump of his left foot, cast sideways glances at the KPV machine gun in tower number one. There was a lighter PK machine gun in tower number two.

Towers number three and four were manned by slovenly Vietnamese conscripts carrying AK-74s.

They had amputated half of Bourke's left foot

in punishment for his last escape attempt. *How many years ago had that been?*

Private First Class Emmanual Rodriquez, Army of the United States, enjoyed the rain beating on his bald head, he gave a toothless grin. He could not remember much about his capture.

His forward fire base had been taking heavy mortar fire, and the gooks were inside the wire. There had been an explosion, blinding white light, then darkness.

Manny had not been able to see the jeering faces as they dragged him through the streets of Hanoi, but he had felt the jabs and kicks and the warm, disgusting spittle on his face.

He had never seen the malevolent faces of his tormentors during his interrogation. *Maybe he was luckier than the rest?*

He had never even contemplated escape. *Where would a blind Mexican escape to in Vietnam? All he dared hope for was death.*

Major Anthony Flyer, AUS, ambled, singing nonsensically. His last lucid thought had been when he had seen the muzzle flash of an old Springfield .03 aimed at his LOACH (Light Observation Helicopter).

He ate, drank and exercised when he was told to do so. The .30 caliber round, fired by an ignorant Asian teenager, was still lodged in his once brilliant brain.

The rest of the small group circled their thirty feet by fifty feet of relative freedom for the allotted forty five minutes, before being returned to the lonely desolation of the solitary tiger cages.

Chapter Eight

1945 local, 3 September
London, England, U.K.
Terry Tanner angled across Trafalgar square weighted down with the various chic', gold roped, shopping bags from Picadelly's best shops. A sallow, hulking figure, with a bowler hat pulled low on his brow, discreetly fell in behind her. The fog was settling into the twilight, and the drizzle, that was London, reduced visibility, forcing the observer closer than he would have liked.

Mrs. Cecil Cedric Tanner III did not notice. Her mind was occupied with her daily purchases, and how the new gown would grace her, still young, body at the embassy dinner this evening.

Her mind was also filled with how much better that new gown would look crumbled on the floor of the foreign attach's bedroom.

The cool evening air stirred her hair. Her nipples hardened as she thought of his hard, pampered, tanned, muscular body. She didn't know where Chad was, nor did she give a tinker's damn.

1800 PST, 3 September
Columbia, Oregon
The battalion chief's wife knew she had to visit the young fireman's widow. *Damn it! Mike should be*

here to do this with me. Where is that son-of-a-bitch? But at least my husband is still alive, or at least I think he is, she thought.

It had been a simple, single alarm structure fire. A utility shed, far enough from the main house not to have done any damage had it burned to the ground. But the young, off duty, probationary fireman had seen the dark, ominous smoke as he arrived in his private vehicle minutes ahead of the first arriving engine.

Before the engine company could perform a forward lay on the nearest hydrant, Carlos Jesus Ortega had kicked in the front door of the smoldering shed. The shed was filled with organic phosphates. The resulting backdraft explosion had blown him four hundred and fifty feet in the air.

The E.R. physician had reported the courageous Hispanic firefighter had most likely been dead before he hit the ground. What had once been a living, breathing human being, with hopes, dreams and a child on the way, now lay in the embalming room of McGirk's funeral parlor.

Now Mrs. Michael Roberts, the Mayor, the Assistant Battalion Chief, and Father Fitzgilroy sat uneasily in the very pregnant young widow's apartment balancing cups of cold coffee on their knees. *Damn it Mike, where are you?*

1645 EST, 3 September
Crandal, Michigan

Christine Murphy found a space in the crowded parking lot for her aging station wagon. She braced herself for her bimonthly sojourn to the A & P. With John gone there were less groceries to buy, but the kids were still voracious. Christine herself didn't have much appetite these days.

She had not heard from John in almost a month. In his last letter he had assured her he would be home as soon as he had finished what he had to finish. It was to late to start doubting him now.

She did not notice the gray-green sedan parked diagonally from her, nor had she noted it's presence all week.

1000 EST, 3 September
HQ, Detroit Police Department,
Detroit, Michigan

Captain Mort Jameson studied the Defense Intelligence Agency credentials, as he tried to appraise their owner,

"What's the DIA's interest in Sergeant Washington? Ah, agent Worthington." he asked.

The agent had close cropped, salt and pepper hair over an ebony face. *Did they send a black spook to a black city to investigate a black cop?* wondered the black police commander.

"We'd like to know his whereabouts. It's a matter of national security involving one of his former military associates," replied the blank faced official.

"He's on extended, compassionate leave, somewhere out west," answered Jameson warily.

Mort and Wade had gone through the academy together. They had walked the mean streets of Detroit, and had eaten dinner with his family a week before they had been buried. He had drank with him, cried with him, and hurt for him. He for damn sure was not going to give him up to this fucking Oreo.

"Could you be more specific Captain Jameson?" came the perfect, prep-school diction. No trace of the 'hood here.

Mort had Wade Washington's mailing address in Billings in his wallet. What he handed agent Worthington was the sergeant's personnel file with the ambiguous L.O.A./Indefinite/Personal reasons. The space for Destination/Temporary address had been left blank.

"Wade Washington is a good cop. He is a decorated veteran of both the Police Department, and the military, and one of the finest men I know. His family was burned alive by a bunch of punk niggers, while he was out trying to protect and serve the few decent black people left in this shit hole. He needed some time and I gave it to him," Jameson said. He snapped the federal credentials closed and tossed them in the general direction of the man from Langely.

"Thank you for your cooperation, Captain," said Worthington. He replaced his I.D. to the inside pocket of his loosely cut jacket. His hand lingered briefly on the butt of his Colt Python, before he smiled a set of perfect capped teeth and exited the squad commander's office.

1200 local, 3 September
Lahina, Maui

Darryl Chvostek had spent long enough in uniform himself to recognize that the two men coming up the dock would have been more comfortable in Navy blue than the bright, loose fitting Aloha shirts. He also recognized the distinctive bulges at their waists. His son had been with Team Six long enough that such visitors no longer surprised the elder Chvostek.

"You gentlemen looking to charter a boat?" Darryl asked heartily.

Both produced Office of Naval Intelligence credentials. Probably linebackers when they were at Annapolis, appraised Harry's father.

"I haven't stolen anything from the Navy in over thirty years," he said.

"What is it Dad?" asked Harrison's comely young bride as she rounded the corner.

Both men ONI men eyed her hot pink thong bikini, that accentuated, rather than covered her firm, golden body.

"Is it about Harry?" she asked.

"No dear, just some tourists. Keep an eye on the bait shop for me, will you?" he answered.

Don't look much like tourists to me, she thought as she turned, giving them a much appreciated view of her bare, gently swaying backside. *Lucky sailor,* they both thought.

"Mr. Chvostek, do you know the current whereabouts of your son; Chvostek, Harrison D. Last duty assignment: Basic Underwater Dive School, Little Creek, Virginia?" asked the Navy cops.

"I know my son's name, and his last duty assignment, SEAL TEAM SIX."

Neither flinched at the mention of the ultra-secret, counter-terrorist unit. "I also know he Retired On Active Duty, and therefore his whereabouts is not the Navy's concern. You can forward his retirement checks to this address."

"Look Mr. Chvostek, we don't mean to hard ass you, we just have a few paper work items to close out in connection with your son's classified duty status," said the smaller, if someone six feet two inches and two hundred and thirty pounds can be called smaller, of the two.

Good cop, bad cop, thought Darryl, *Interesting.*

"Just told me he needed some time alone. Said he'd be traveling and in touch. So far, haven't heard from him," replied Chvostek.

"Well if you do have contact, please have him get in touch with the Office of Naval Intelligence at Pearl," said the bigger one. The small one offered a business card bearing a fouled anchor in raised gold.

0850 EST, 3 September
The White House, Washington, D.C.

Cindy Carmicheal was early for her appointment with Senator Paul Burley, chairman of the Arms Appropriation sub-committee. She had not heard from Judd. She had tried to occupy her troubled mind by working even more than usual.

Senator Burley had given her a fairly open door to his office. Over the years he had proven to be a valuable contact.

She suspected he would especially like to offer her an open door to his bedroom.

She had found that being a spectacular female was a real asset on the hill.

Though there had been many opportunities, and several blatant offers, power was an aphrodisiac, she had never been tempted. Well, maybe tempted, but never tested.

Not even when Judd was away for extended periods, as he often was. He was simply too much man, and she loved him too much to ever stray.

"I want that report, and the DIA/CIA report, including the President's reply in front of the Select House Committee on POW/MIA affairs before close of business today," grumbled the tall Senator from Louisiana, into the phone. He slammed the receiver into it's cradle, and slid the red bordered file into his top desk drawer as Cindy entered the plushly carpeted office.

The mahogany paneled walls were bare save for the framed display of Combat Infantry Badge centered over the "Indian Head" shoulder patch of the Second Infantry Division. A Silver Star medal flanked one side, and a Purple Heart medal was on the other.

"Mrs. Carmicheal," he beamed as he came from behind his massive desk and extended a large, rough hand.

Nice, craggy face, good shoulders, big hands, thought Cindy, *if I wasn't already married to the best...*

0700 local, 3 September
Phu Duc Prison, DPRV

Colonel Bat Ky had been commandant of the prison for more years than he cared to remember; ever since an American claymore had destroyed most of his left leg. It had been a safe, comfortable billet. A fitting reward for a Hero of the Revolution.

There had not been an escape attempt in years. Hanoi had not explained why they were suddenly reinforcing defenses with a Commando Attack Unit of the elite 325th Light Infantry. They had also started construction on an expanded mine field. He wondered if it was all related to the collapse of their big brother the Union of Soviet Socialist Republics.

Both Giap and Ho had taught life, like war was

in a constant state of flux and therefore change would be beneficial. He knew this could not be considered a personal criticism. He would personally check the new security and establish control.

0700 local, 3 September
Vigilant Leader Labor and Reeducation Camp, DPRV

Tran watched the old "six by six" truck unload the platoon of young troopers from the 325th Light Infantry. *Why, suddenly, extra security. Certainly his "cattle" did not warrant extra guards. They only needed to be herded. As they had for years now,* he thought.

Lieutenant Commander Rudolf F. Heron, USN noted the troops arriving. He had not seen regular Army troops, moving as a coordinated military unit since '74 of '75. *Wonder what year this is?*

His fellow inmates had dwindled to twenty nine men. No one spoke much anymore, nothing to say, besides, it took too much of their precious energy.

Even though they tried to supplement their sparse diet with insects, roots and small rodents; working the fields burned most of the kilo calories consumed.

Sometimes, this area of Northern Vietnam reminded Heron of his home in Georgia. At least he thought it did, he really couldn't remember.

1830 EST, 3 September
Pope Air Force Base, North Carolina

Colonel Marcus Lee Biggs, AUS descended the ramp of the huge C-133, his CAR-15 slung over his right shoulder and his bulging duffel balanced on his left. The sleeve of his camo BDUs rolled to reveal bulging biceps. His forest green beret set low on his steel gray head. His hard, cold eyes penetrated the dusk, looking for his bride.

The men of Delta Detachment trailed behind their commander. They had just returned from extended training in the Canal Zone at the Army's Jungle Warfare Training Center and all looked forward to a much deserved leave.

His eyes found Betsy. The tall, statuesque brunette stood out in her bright yellow slicker. His battered, craggy face broke into a lopsided grin as she worked her way toward him.

"Hey soldier, wanna mess around? Fuckie, suckie?" she purred as she pressed herself into her husband. She ignored the various bulges and bumps of his combat gear. That is, all but one bulge of his combat gear. "Does that mean you missed me or are you carrying a concealed weapon?" she whispered in his ear as she nibbled on the lobe.

"Both," he replied huskily into the perfume of her hair.

As they walked out to their aging Bronco II he asked, "is that slicker new? Looks good on you."

"Uhh huhh, got it when I visited mom out in Wyoming, it's a perfect outfit."

On the way home he found out just how perfect the slicker was. His bride of twenty years was wearing the slicker, high heels, nylons and a garter belt, PERIOD.

She had worked hard to maintain her cheerleader's body, and loved it when Marc appreciated it. *He really knows how to appreciate it,* she thought.

He kept her climbing the seat with his talented hands, during the short ride to base housing.

By the time they reached the brick duplex, she

wanted more than his hand. Much more. She pushed him on to the floor of the front room, tore the buttons from his trousers and mounted him. He totally forgot the obnoxious beeper sounding on his belt as Betsy pulled him inside her, and inside her, and inside her. They were both exploding in a mind wrenching orgasm when the pager's insistent summons drilled it's way into his consciousness.

1130 EST, 3 September
Langley, Virginia

Richard Markam sat at his desk staring at the roster from Phu Duc Prison. He also had field reports spread out before him, trailing J.D. Carmicheal and his 'Nam buddies. He knew that son-of-a-bitch was up to something, and these documents were all connected with that Goddamn POW thing. He hadn't quite pieced it together. Now the President had placed Delta on yellow alert, and the Rapid Deployment Force of the 82nd. Airborne had been ordered on standby. An AMPHIB Group of the Pacific Fleet had changed course to subtly head toward the South China Sea. *What the hell is Caldwell up to, exactly?*

He lit another cigarette and pulled out the pint of Old Crow. His wife and his doctor had been trying to get him to quit both.

Chapter Nine

0500 MST, 5 September
"Star Corral", Montana

The C-130 lumbered into the breaking day. A steady downpour had begun an hour before first light. Team Bougainvillea were strapped in their respective seats, alone with their individual thoughts, hopes and prayers. The next twenty four hours would decide their collective fate, and the fate of seventeen fellow Americans, long ago abandoned by the very country they had served. Judd Carmicheal wondered if the mission would lower the number of POW/MIAs, or merely add ten new names to the two thousand six hundred and sixty six unaccounted for. He also wondered if there would ever be a similar mission into Laos and the USSR/UER?

Frank Morningstar trimmed the flaps and set the auto-pilot, baromctric setting, and magnetic compass manually. Chad Tanner double checked the settings as he fed them into the on board computers, factoring in their refueling point, drop zone and return coordinates. There would be no need to activate the newly installed, sophisticated Electronic Counter Measures until they were well over the South China Sea and approaching the air space of the Peoples Republic of China. All instruments were in the green. Chad wished he felt as confident as Frank appeared.

"Sit back and enjoy the ride, doze off for a while, the auto's got it," said the Sioux. *Hard to tell what an Indian is thinking*, thought the Brit. *Wonder what the hell that white eyed Limey is thinking?* thought Morningstar.

"You got a wife Frank?" Chad finally asked.

"Several, how about you?" Frank replied.

"In a manner of speaking," was Chad's terse comment. He applied protractor and compass to the map spread on the navigator's table behind his left hand seat, facing away from the native American.

He was now peering directly into the red glow of the cabin. He considered his fellow team members.

It's the fourth of July, or maybe Labor Day; Diane Washington is flipping burgers on the grill, sun is blazing, sky is cloudless, and kids were playing on the swings on Belle Isle. Belle Isle is a small patch of peace, tranquillity and nature situated in the Detroit River between the United States and their nonviolent neighbor to the south. Wade was stretched out in the grass with a cold Stroh's to his lips. Mort and Susie Jameson were pushing their kids on the merry-go-round. Suddenly, inexplicably, Diane, Joey and Maggie burst into flames. They were screaming. Wade was stuck in the grass, like quicksand. No one seemed to notice, his friends did not see the horror. They were laughing on the merry-go-round. "Someone fucking help them! Oh God

HELP! " he screamed. Someone was shaking Wade hard, "Wade, Wade. Buddy, wake up. You're

O.K., come on." He felt John Murphy's big Irish hand sting his face, turning the ebony to a peculiar shade of crimson purple. Tears ran unabashedly down Wade's cheeks.

Washington's day-mare had roused the others from their reverie.

Murphy's mind had been on Son Tay. That time his officially sanctioned team had lain mattresses on the deck of huge CH-34 Chinook helicopters. The "Shit hooks" had deliberately crash landed into the prison compound, only to find that the POWs had been moved less than seventy two hours before. Security had either been blown on that one, or someone above his pay grade had decided to turn it into a dog and pony show for the constituents back home, without pissing off the gooks too badly.

When the team had returned to the world they had made unauthorized shoulder patches for themselves, bearing a mushroom with the initials, K.I.T.D.F.O.B.S. (Kept In Total Darkness, Fed Only Bull Shit). They had all worn the patches in '75 at the Fairmont Hotel in San Francisco when H. Ross Perot had hosted a party with John Wayne for the returning POWs and the members of Operation Kingpin.

John Wayne had awoken the general manager and had him open the kitchen at O dark thirty to feed the hungry, mostly inebriated, POWs and Son Tay Raiders. The senior chef had personally appeared in his pajamas and tall white cap to honor, "some real Americans", to quote the Duke.

Harrison Chvostek studied his fellow warriors in the artificial dawn of the cargo plane's interior. *Their one last mission, one mission too much?* He would miss Maui, he would especially miss his bride of three months. *Wonder if the guys we're going after still miss anything, or even remember anything back home?*

"Hey doc, What's it like in the Emergency room?" asked Moses Tipton.

"A lot like this," replied Reynolds.

Thomas Darrow, National Security Advisor to the President of the United States, had no idea what the fuck he was doing on this mission. Carmicheal had steadfastly refused, until the NSA had told him the painful story of his son's remains coming home last year in a brass container, the size and shape of a shoe box.

The Army Forensics Laboratory at Schofield Barracks, Hawaii had enclosed a letter of authentication, but Darrow was not convinced.

When his wife lay, dying of lung cancer, at Bethesda Naval Hospital, her last words had been, "Mikey is not dead. He will come home, and not in a damn box." He also knew the President would have his balls for lunch for this stunt, but it was something he had to do.

"Everyone check your personal equipment, then get some shuteye," commanded Judd, knowing how impossible the latter command would be.

1130 MST, 5 September
"Star Corral", Montana

The blue and white Lear jet settled on the tarmac and rolled most of the length of the runway, before coming to a stop at the end where Chad Tanner's Citation was hangered. The hatch opened and Richard A. Markam, Director of the Defense Intelligence Agency, and his entourage of flunkies emerged. One look told him the camp was deserted. He began a search to confirm his suspicions.

The searchcrs found hundreds of spent catridge cases in the area set up to resemble a prison of some sort. In the main lodge they found computers, easels, and a sand model resembling either a prison or military compound, perhaps both. Numerous pin holes in the paneling suggested a display or more likely maps had been attached.

"Sir, look at this," one of the Director's crewcut minions exclaimed, handing him a photo retrieved from behind a cushion of an overstuffed leather sofa. Markam held an eight by ten black and white photo he knew to be a COMSAT picture of an alleged prison camp in Vietnam. He recognized it from J.D. Carmicheal's last report on the subject.

He self consciously realized his hands were trembling.

"Son-of-a-bitch!" he muttered as he headed for his aircraft.

"Patch me through to The White House, Priority One," he ordered the startled co-pilot/navigator. His men were still searching the compound for other clues to confirm what Markam already knew in his heart to be the situation.

Goddamn his insubordinate soul, anyway!

1745 EST, 5 September
The Oval Office

"Mr. Director, I find it extremely difficult to believe that an agent of the Defense Intelligence Agency and a loyal American took it upon himself to launch a renegade raid into the territory of a sovereign nation." Hiram Caldwell spoke calmly into the secure, scrambled, speaker phone dominating one corner of his massive oaken desk, as he thumbed the buzzer to summon Thomas Darrow into the inner-sanctum of the Oval Office.

"This is a diplomatic nightmare, Mr. President. We must notify the State Department ASAP. We must also alert the Vietnamese Premier and the President of the UER. They must be made to understand that this was a purely civilian adventurer's folly, and does not reflect the official policy of these United States. It must not be construed as an attack on a foreign power," the DIA chief stammered. "As soon as I sign off I'll notify the CIA," he continued.

The NSA's secretary scribbled a note stating that Mr. Darrow had not yet arrived at his office. The President acknowledged with a curt nod, and waited for her to depart before responding to the DIA Director,

"Mr. Markam, consider yourself under executive order to hold this information strictly confidential. It is a matter of extreme national security. You will NOT notify the State Department. You will NOT notify the CIA. You will NOT notify the Democratic Peoples Republic of Vietnam, nor the Union of Eurasian Republics. You will tell NO ONE without My express permission. IS THAT PERFECTLY CLEAR?"

"But Mr. President –," stammered the bureaucrat.

"IS THAT PERFECTLY CLEAR? MR. MARKAM?" the PUS asked firmly.

"Uhh, yes Sir, I'll return to Washington immediately and report to your office directly," Markam conceded.

"You do that Mr. Markam," Caldwell concluded.

The pilot was already pre-flighting the aircraft and feeding the coordinates for D.C. into the inertial navigation computer. He did not need the DIA chief's curt reminder that the previous transmission had been of a top secret nature. He had been a DIA pilot for over fifteen years, the last five as the Director's personal air chauffeur.

The Lear was streaking due east at forty nine thousand feet, and over three hundred miles per hour. It was less than forty five minutes after touch down at Team Bougainvillea's staging area. *Should have shot that bastard years ago*, was one of Markam's more charitable thoughts as he considered his former SAC.

1750 EST, 5 September
The Oval Office

Can't believe that pompous ass would compromise the slim chance any POWs can be brought home, thought the President as he made some rapid command decisions. He picked up the scrambler handset and flipped the switch connecting him to the world wide military net.

"Get me Colonel Biggs, he should be on standby at The Ranch."

Within minutes they were connected. The scrambler distorted but could not disguise the Delta commander's gravely voice.

"Marcus, this is Homeplate. Activate Eagle. Execute on my command only," ordered the most powerful man in the free world.

1755 EST, 5 September
Camp McCall, North Carolina

Biggs had only barely gotten out his, "Affirmative

Sir," before securing the net and heading for the Operations Ready Room. The klaxon he had activated would summon the "On Alert" Detachment members to the Ready Room.

Eagle was an operation they had all rehearsed for months on end. It was a plan to rescue American subjects from an armed enemy on foreign soil.

The last such operation had ended disastrously at Desert one.

The duty communications sergeant, Wayne Matthews, had just pulled a coded transmission from the telex and was inserting it into the decoding apparatus as his C.O. entered. The clear transmission emerged seconds later:

to: Commanding Delta Detachment, USA/SF Special Operations Command, Ft. Bragg, North Carolina, USA

subject: Operation Eagle

clearance: Top Secret/Eyes Only/Need to Know

message: Unit directed to proceed at all possible speed to rendezvous w/USS Guadalcanal (LH-4) coordinate with elements of RDF/82nd.ABN Rescue mission American citizens. Location to be specified next transmission. Equipment and personnel per T.O. Execute ONLY on executive order, per code of date. THIS IS NOT A DRILL. REPEAT. THIS IS NOT A DRILL.

authority: Commander-in-Chief, current position LH-4 follows. DESTROY AFTER READING. end transmission. 1802 Hrs GMT, 5 September.

When Colonel Biggs fed the coordinates into the Ready Room computer he was surprised to see the South China Sea come up on the screen.

The 144th. Special Forces Aviation Company

had already fed the coordinates into the MH-30, Pave-Lo, helicopters on board inertial navigation and arranged air-to-air refueling out of Subic Bay.

Thirty Delta Detachment troopers with full combat gear were filling three unmarked, turbojet helicopters, as the turbines wound up. Saddle up, lock and load, thought the Green Beret colonel as he ducked into the rotor wash.

0300 local, 5 September
USS McGowen (CVS-66), Pacific Ocean

Major Anthony Wayne, AUS/3rd of the 75th Ranger Battallion/RDF/82nd.ABN stood on the flight deck of the Enterprise Class aircraft carrier and studied the Eyes Only telex. The message was essentially the same as Colonel Biggs had received moments earlier, and several hundred miles away.

The location of the planned rescue was not yet specified, but the McGowen was to rendezvous with the Guadalcanal in the international waters of the South China Sea. Those waters had become considerably friendlier since the collapse of the USSR.

He had thirty six Airborne Ranger, snake eaters on board. Ready, willing and able to perform a snatch on hostile soil. Most had been with him in Panama and Grenada and had served with distinction. Major Wayne was ready.

0700 PST, 6 September
AC-130 Talon, over the Pacific Ocean

"Feet wet," announced Morningstar as he watched the California coast pass beneath his wings. "Next stop Phillips 66," he told Chad Tanner.

"Sure hope the petrol's where it's supposed to be. Never was one for swimming," answered the taciturn Brit.

"No worries mate," quipped Frank.

Judd appeared with two steaming mugs of coffee.

"You really think we're gonna do this thing boss?" asked the Sioux.

"Oh we're gonna do it. The question is, are we going to do it and live to tell about it?" answered the C.O.

Both men gave him a thumbs up.

0900 GMT, 6 September
AC-130 Talon, over the Pacific Ocean

"Fuckin A!" exclaimed both pilots as they spotted the C-133 configured as an airborne refueling station.

"Boxcar to Guernsey," Frank transmitted on the agreed upon guard channel.

"Line up with my tit, Boxcar," the tanker replied as the refueling cone snaked out from the tail boom, piloted by a young Air Force Technical Sergeant who seldom knew the destination of the aircraft he fueled.

This is one of the most nerve wracking airborne procedures a pilot can experience; all four pilots concentrated on the task at hand.

Frank Morningstar disengaged the auto pilot as Chad Tanner poised both hands over the yoke, ready to assist in any sudden pitch and yaw. Frank maneuvered his lumbering aircraft into position as the sergeant sought it's probe. All three men were sweating profusely in their air conditioned confines.

The cockpit crew of the tanker perspired also as they tried to maintain slow, level flight against the buffeting created by the close proximity of the Talon. Finally came the reassuring "clunk" of probe/cone engagement and the refueling Christmas trees in both aircraft went to full green.

"Drink's on the way, Boxcar," transmitted Guernsey.

Thousands of pounds of high grade, JP-4, aviation fuel was transferred to the thirsty C-130 in minutes. The two aircraft continued, high over the Pacific Ocean like a cow and her calf. Though this calf was almost as big as it's mother.

"See you on our return, Guernsey," said Frank with considerably more confidence than he felt.

0900 GMT, 6 September
USS Guadalcanal, Pacific Ocean

The Tarawa class helicopter assault ship prepared to accept the three arriving Pave-Los bearing the members of Delta Detachment.

Captain Nathaniel Zelinski greeted Colonel Biggs as he dismounted from the ominous appearing black helicopter.

"Permission to come aboard," said the Army commander as he saluted the colors and then the ship's captain. As Zelinski returned the colonel's salute he handed him a thick manila envelope with the distinctive red slashed border denoting a Top Secret dispatch.

"My men and my ship are at your disposal, Colonel. My crew will assist your men in getting settled below decks," said the Captain.

0915 GMT, 6 September
ward room, USS Guadalcanal

"I'll be a humpback monkey fucker," Marcus Biggs

said to the empty room as he spilled the contents of the envelope onto the gray metal desk. *Now just give us the GO!* he thought.

His thoughts were interrupted by the knock of Captain Zelinski, "You tell me where you need them and I'll give your mission MG-CAP. Between my Cobras and the McGowen's 14s and 15s we can give you all the air cover you want."

"I just read my orders from the man; and I say it's about time. A lot of us have a real personal interest in this mission," continued the naval commander.

"IF we get the launch command," replied Biggs.

Chapter Ten

1900 EST, 6 September
DIA Headquarters
Markam's fingers danced on the keyboard as he prepared for his meeting with the President. He had now identified the photo recovered from the Montana staging area as Phu Duc Prison, located in northern Vietnam, near the Chinese border. According to J.D. Carmicheal's report, live Americans were allegedly held there. He had also obtained the purloined roster from the UER which also identified American POWs at Phu Duc. He was convinced that an armed assault by Carmicheal's Commandos was imminent.

As the DIA chief checked off names on the yellow legal pad, he punched up their files on the powerful agency computer, which was interconnected with every government agency in the country:

name: Carmicheal, Judd Davenport

occupation: SAC Atlantic region, DIA

DOB: 27 April 1943, Bloomfield, Indiana, USA

military service: Army of the United States / Special Forces (Airborne)

rank: colonel

overseas duty: Dominican Republic, Laos, Republic of Vietnam, Iran, Panama

awards and decorations: Distinguished Service Cross, Distinguished Service Medal, Silver Star, Bronze Star w/'V', Purple Heart w/cluster, Presidential Unit Citation, Vietnam Service, Vietnam Campaign, Armed Forces Expeditionary Medal, Combat Infantry Badge (second award), Master Parachute Badge w/combat star, USN Basic Underwater Dive Badge, Small Arms expert, Rifle sharpshooter, Pathfinder Badge, Ranger tab, Jungle Expert, SEAR instructor, Leadership Award, Vietnamese Medal of Honor, Vietnamese Cross of Gallantry second class w/palms, Vietnamese Ranger, National Defense medal, DIA Meritorious Service.

military occupational specialty: 61-N/4/P/S

current address: Georgetown, Virginia, USA

A familiar photo occupied the left side of the monitor screen.

Markam keyed in the next name on his roster:

name: Murphy, John Lawrence

occupation: self employed, over the road trucker

DOB: 24 June 1945, Marquette, Michigan, USA

military service: Army of the United States / Special Forces (Airborne)

rank: Master Sergeant

overseas duty: Cuba, Laos, Republic of Vietnam, Iran, Grenada, Panama.

awards and decorations: Silver Star, Bronze Star w/'V', Presidential Unit Citation, Purple Heart w/cluster, Army Commendation w/'V', Vietnam Service, Vietnam Campaign, Vietnamese Cross of Gallantry 1st. Class, Armed Forces Expeditionary Medal, Good Conduct Medal (six awards), Combat Infantry Badge (second award), Master Parachute Badge w/combat star, USN Basic Underwater Dive Badge, Pathfinder Badge, Jungle expert, Ranger tab, National Defense Medal.

M.O.S.: 61-N/4/P/S

current address: Crandal, Michigan, USA

The photo was of a stocky, craggy faced Caucasian of obvious Irish descent. His red hair was turning silver at the temples and he sported a bushy, gunfighter's mustache.

Richard Markam entered the next name from the yellow pad:

name: Washington, Wade Carver

occupation: police officer

DOB: 19 January 1947, Detroit, Michigan

military service: Army of the United States / Special Forces (Airborne)

rank: Staff Sergeant

overseas duty: Laos, Republic of Vietnam.

awards and decorations: Bronze Star w/'V', Purple Heart Presidential Unit Citation, Soldier's Medal w/'V', Armed Forces Expeditionary Medal, Combat Infantry Bade, Senior Parachute Badge, Ranger tab, Vietnamese Cross of Gallantry 3rd Class, Vietnam Service, Vietnam Campaign, National Defense, Good Conduct Medal.

M.O.S.: 11-B/P/S

current address: Detroit, Michigan, USA

The grainy photo was of a slightly over weight black male with steel gray, close cropped, wiry hair and a somewhat battered face. He was wearing the uniform of a Detroit Patrol Sergeant.

The DIA Director was becoming more agitated as he keyed in the next name on his list:

name: Roberts, Michael James

occupation: Fire Service Officer

DOB: 17 July 1944, Portland, Oregon

military service: U.S. Marine Corps / (Airborne Reconnaissance)

rank: Gunnery Sergeant

overseas duty: Cuba, Dominican Republic, Republic of Vietnam, Grenada.

awards and decorations: Navy Cross, Silver Star, Purple Heart, Combat Action Medal, Vietnam Service, Vietnam Campaign, National Defense, Armed Forces Expeditionary Medal, Naval Parachutist, USN Basic Underwater Dive Badge, Small arms expert, Rifle expert.

M.O.S.: 0311/P/R

current address: Columbia, Oregon, USA

The computer generated likeness depicted a middle-aged, ruggedly handsome individual wearing a Fire Officer's uniform.

On to the next bastard, thought Markam as his fingers played the keyboard:

name: Reynolds, David Raffael

occupation: M.D.

DOB: 11 March 1946, San Antonio, Texas, USA

military service: Army of the United States / Special Forces (Airborne)

rank: Staff Sergeant

overseas duty: Laos, Republic of Vietnam

awards and decorations: Distinguished Service Cross, Bronze Star w/'V', Purple Heart, Armed Forces Expeditionary Medal, Presidential Unit Citation, Vietnamese Civil Action, Combat Medic Badge, Senior Parachutist Badge, Ranger tab, Jungle Expert, Vietnam Service , Vietnam Campaign, National Defense, Good Conduct Medal, Rifle sharpshooter, Small Arms expert.

M.O.S.: 91-C/P/S

current address: El Paso, Texas, USA

The accompanying photo was of a lanky, sandy

haired Caucasian with a seamed, lèathery face and stark blue eyes.

Markam entered the next name:

name: Chvostek, Harrison Daniel

occupation: Sr. Chief Petty Officer, USN (ROAD)

DOB: 6 June 1943, Pearl Harbor, Hawaii

military service: U.S. Navy / SEAL (Airborne)

overseas duty: Laos, Republic of Vietnam, Grenada, classified European and Asian stations.

awards and decorations: Navy Cross, Silver Star (second award), Armed Forces Expeditionary Medal, Presidential Unit Citation, Vietnamese Cross of Gallantry 1st Class w/palms, Naval Master Parachutist, Master Underwater Dive Badge, Special Warfare Badge, Good Conduct Medal (six awards), Combat Action, Vietnam Service, Vietnam Campaign, National Defense, Purple Heart w/cluster.

M.O.S.: 0324-P/S

current address: Lahina, Maui, Hawaii, USA

Another, middle-aged, capable appearing, professional was depicted alongside the raw data.

Richard Markam was halfway down his roster:

name: Tipton, Moses Washington

occupation: unemployed

DOB: 14 February 1947, Fairhope, Alabama

military service: U.S. Navy / SEAL (Airborne)

overseas duty: Republic of Vietnam

rank: Petty Officer First Class

awards and decorations: Silver Star (third award), Purple Heart w/cluster, Combat Action, Marksmanship Award, Vietnam Service, Vietnam Campaign, National Defense, Special Warfare Badge, Basic Underwater Dive Badge.

M.O.S.: 0391-P/S

current address: unknown

The photo shown was over thirty years old and depicted a very young black man with high cheekbones, strong jaw and deep set eyes.

The next name on the list had caused Markam to violate the integrity of both Department of Immigration and United Kingdom files. He had incurred some heavy debts to obtain the following information:

name: Tanner, Cecil Cedrick III

occupation: rancher

DOB: 5 May 1948, Sheffield, England, UK

military service: Royal Air Force / Special Air Service

rank: Wing Commander

overseas duty: Rhodesia, South Africa, Falkland Islands, classified European and Asian stations.

awards and decorations: Victoria Cross, Cross of St. George, Valorous Service, Meritorious Service, Distinguished Service Order, Order of The Knights of the Regent, Rhodesian Campaign, South African Defense, Falkland Campaign, Senior Pilot, Senior Parachutist.

M.O.S.: 32-P-456-S/A

current address: Billings , Montana, USA

The grim faced British subject on the passport photo did not look like a rancher to Richard Markam. He looked like what he was: one of the world's premier special operations officers. The SAS was the prototype commando unit in the free world.

Rubbing the two day stubble on his chin, Markam keyed in the last name, it too had cost him some favors:

name: Morningstar, Frank Romero

occupation: pilot

DOB: 8 August 1947, Spearfish, South Dakota, USA

military service: none

Civilian Department of Defense service: Air America/Central Intelligence Agency

overseas duty: Laos, Cambodia, Republic of Vietnam, Thailand, Central America, classified European and Asian stations

awards and decorations: CIA citation for Distinguished Service

rank: command pilot

M.O.S.: N/A

current address: unknown

This photo was of a distinguished appearing native American with silver hair framing a square, mahogany face.

"O.K., that's the gang," announced Markam to the empty office. He gathered the print-outs to include with Carmicheal's POW/MIA report.

He then addressed the prison roster and began feeding the seventeen names into the computer.

The machine whirred and hummed as the "201" files of missing service men began to appear on the color monitor. The laser jet printer began delivering hard copies.

"HOLY SHIT!" exclaimed Markam as he hit the "pause" and "zoom" buttons simultaneously. The glowing white letters in the center of the magenta screen read:

Darrow, Michael Thomas, Captain, U.S. Air Force.

Missing-In-Action Area of Operations Haiphong Harbor, DPRV, Operation Rolling Thunder, 15 July

1970, next of kin: Thomas Darrow.

It was the third name on the roster of War Criminals held at Phu Duc.

He was to meet with President Caldwell at twenty hundred hours.

2000 EST, 6 September
National Command Center, Washington, D.C.

Hiram Caldwell had again assembled the Joint Chiefs as well as the directors of CIA, DIA, and FBI. His NSA was nowhere to be found.

He noted that Richard Alexander Markam was particularly florid this evening. He took a sip of black coffee, cleared his throat and addressed the auspicious group.

"Gentlemen, it's time I brought you up to speed regarding recent developments in the POW/MIA issue," he continued, "As you may or may not be aware; we have received a document from the Unified Eurasian Republic identifying live American prisoners in the Democratic Peoples Republic of Vietnam. It is dated this year."

The assembled officers sat silently, waiting for the other shoe to drop. Markam's knuckles were white as he clutched the thick file he had compiled, awaiting the President's next pronouncement.

"I have deployed Delta Detachment, and elements of the Rapid Deployment Force as well as an Amphibious Assault Group within striking distance of the mainland of Vietnam. They are on yellow alert for a possible rescue mission. I ask the Joint Chiefs to bring our readiness posture to DefCon Three."

The Chief of Naval Operations rose to his feet,

"Mr. President, that could be construed as an overt act of war, the War Powers Act states," President Caldwell interrupted, "Admiral, I do not want to go to war anymore than you do, but, the collapse of the Soviet Union removes any threat of serious reprisal from that quarter. Intelligence advises that the DPRV does not have nuclear capability. China will not intervene. If live POWs are verified, I will go get them!"

A tall, slender, career Marine with gold Naval Parachute wings topping six rows of ribbons, centered over a single pale blue ribbon dusted with stars, pushed back his chair, rose, cleared his throat and spoke, "Mr. President, two questions, one, is verification possible in an expeditious fashion; two, what can the Marine Corps do to help?"

The President spoke directly to the Commandant Marine Corps, noting the black ribbon with the red and white ends amidst the more colorful ones. Also noting that the brother Marine was a fellow Medal of Honor winner. "General, a covert mission is underway, even as we speak. When and if the field commander verifies the existence of live American subjects, we will launch a reconnaissance in force on two suspect location in the DPRV. We will then demand that the Department of State and the United Nations World Court to bring the Vietnamese government to a full accounting of all POW/MIAs."

An Air Force four star began a slow, quiet applause which grew and was picked up by the entire room.

Even Richard A. Markam found the enthusiasm infectious and joined in what soon became a thunderous ovation.

Hiram Caldwell, President of the United States of America, Congressional Medal of Honor winner, rose,

"Gentlemen, I am sorry I was not able to involve you before this point in time. Diplomatic and security restraints prohibited that. The mission in progress is officially unofficial and unsanctioned, a strictly civilian enterprise. If it fails, it shall forever remain so.

The events that have occurred in this room, as always, remain in this room. The individual unit commanders will be notified as to the go/no-go status of further action as soon as I have reached that decision."

A Marine guard in Dress Blues entered with a message which the President read, and then adjourned the meeting and left through the door leading to the Oval Office elevator.

Chapter Eleven

0100 GMT, 5 September
over the coast of the Peoples Republic of China

Judd Carmicheal checked the lithium batteries in his satellite burst transmitter and then jacked a 5.56mm, copper-jacketed round into his CAR-15 and flipped the selector lock to full auto and thumbed the safety on. "Hook up, OBAs on, stand in the door," he ordered.

Eight middle-aged commandos, weighed down with full combat gear, strapped oxygen masks to their camouflaged faces, lowered their NVDs, and clipped snap-hooks to the overhead cable running the length of the cargo bay.

It was impossible to tell if their thoughts were profound or profane. Even if you could have seen their faces in the red glow of the aircraft interior, behind the Night Vision Devices, Oxygen Breathing Apparatus, and camo paint, you would only have seen a quiet determination and resolution.

As the rear ramp of the C-130 opened to the rarefied atmosphere of twenty eight thousand feet, the stick checked each other's parachute harness; tugging here, adjusting there. A tap on the Kevlar helmet signaled all was A-O.K.

Mike Roberts assured the accuratized Barnett crossbow was strapped securely to his reserve 'chute, resting on his lower abdomen. The hardwood quarrels were secure in a pouch on his ALICE webbing. "Three Roger," he transmitted.

John Murphy was in the number eight position. He wondered if the bureaucrat in the number seven slot would freeze in the door. Somehow he doubted it. *That old man seems almost on a religious mission. 'A mission from God,' as the Blues Brothers would say.* "Eight go."

I wonder if Murph' is supposed to kick me in the ass if I hesitate? thought Thomas Darrow as he snugged the groin harness one notch tighter. As he looked into the jet black sky he wondered if somewhere down there his son was rotting in prison. *Well, someone's son damn sure is.*

"Seven go."

"Six Roger," replied Moses Tipton to his commander's inquiry over the VLF inter-team head set. *'To all the girls I've loved,'* he thought as he shifted the weight of the ParaCommando main 'chute harnessed to his broad back.

Dave Reynolds watched the slowly evolving night sky as it revealed a thumbnail sliver of moon. *A commando's sky, maybe Somebody is on our side after all.*

He could feel the perceptible slowing down as the cargo ramp, acting like a huge air brake, increased the Talon's drag. *Are we jumping into history or obscurity?* Dr. Reynolds waxed prophetic as he reflexively answered, "Five Roger."

"Four go," answered Harrison Chvostek into his helmet's mouthpiece. "Oh, I miss my little grass shack in La Hina Ka Nui, Maui," he sang softly as he punched the button on his chronometer to start the mission countdown to Zero hour.

Wade Washington stared at his commander's back, silhouetted in the open maw of the AC-130. The jump light just beyond Judd's right shoulder glowed red at the moment. *One last time to kick ass and take names for the good ol' U.S. of A. What the fuck, maybe I'll be seeing you soon Babe,* he thought as he chambered a round into his M-16.

The thin air at twenty eight thousand feet buffeted Judd as he stood in the cargo bay staring at the jump light.

"Stand in the door," he commanded.

The eight man stick shuffled rearward in lockstep until their commander's boots were on the edge of the ramp. There were only a smattering of stars above, and solid cloud cover below them. *good night to jump. A good night to die.*

Morningstar and Tanner were busy in the cockpit trying to keep the ungainly aircraft airborne, just above stall speed against the drag of the rear cargo ramp.

They both held the yokes firmly to maintain straight and level flight as Team Bougainvillea approached the designated drop zone. They had activated the ECM before entering PRC airspace.

They had noted random search radar, but nothing locked on to their unauthorized presence. Both men were keenly aware of the multiple SAM installations aimed at their vulnerable underbelly.

The FLIR did not warn of any challengers as of yet. Both knew they could not survive the interest of even one lone patrolling MIG-34.

When the onboard computer signaled they were over the specified coordinates, Frank toggled the switch to change the cabin jump light to green.

He imagined he could feel the team leaving the relative protection of the airframe, *good luck guys, see you on the ground, I hope.*

The short stick exited the aircraft. They were buffeted by the thin night air and the wash from the quad turboprops, as one by one the stepped into space.

They could not see the ground twenty eight thousand feet below, beneath the clouds. As each counted, they waited for the almost imperceptible tug of the static line deploying their pilot 'chute, followed by the gut wrenching, shoulder straining deceleration from one hundred and twenty feet per second of terminal velocity that signaled deployment of their black ParaCommando airfoil.

With it's cargo dispensed, the AC-130 went to full throttle, climbed, and began a lazy 360 degree turn.

It would attempt a surreptitious landing to coordinate with the ground team attack when signaled by J.D.

They knew the big cumbersome aircraft would be most vulnerable on the ground. The plan was to keep this window of opportunity to a minimum required for the task at hand.

The eight commandos hung suspended over the Peoples Republic of China as they checked canopies to assure proper blossom, and risers to assure tangle free operation. They then checked each other's relative position. They were unable to see the landscape, but steered by compass and altimeter fastened to their reserve 'chutes, resting on their laps.

As the team appeared to properly deployed and heading in the right direction, Judd did not use the VLF intercom. It was highly unlikely that a ground listening post could detect the Very Low Frequency communication, but it seemed prudent to keep voice traffic to a minimum.

As they traveled laterally, catching the warm ground up drafts, their compass's told them they were crossing into hostile territory. Not that the PRC would appreciate their intrusion anymore than the DPRV.

Passing through the cloud cover, their NVDs began to identify the eerie green shapes of the low lying mountains which indicated the border. They knew they were really in the shit now.

Wade Washington slipped right to allow his compass to align on the coordinates which would land him near the equipment cache. *If it's where it's supposed to be.*

The last time he had set foot in Vietnam he had sworn never to return. *Now here I am, a fat, dumb cop, blissfully floating into gookville, just as if I had good sense. Must be even dumber than I look,* he thought as the lush vegetation rushed toward his jungle boots. *Wonder if they still have panthers in these mountains?*

Moses Tipton kept the small cat's eye stripe on the back of J.D.'s Kevlar "Fritz" helmet in sight, as he steered toward the drop zone. Inexplicably, his thoughts were on his aging parents and their Alabama farm. He hadn't seen, nor communicated with them in many years.

Goddamn cramp, thought John Murphy as he worked his foot in the tightly laced boot. The spring steel embedded in the rubber sole limited flexibility.

Well here I am again, happy as a shit eating

dog, just as stupid, thought Dr. Dave Reynolds as he lightly fingered the trigger guard of his M-16, and watched the ground rush to meet him through his NVD.

This was Thomas Darrow's fourth parachute jump in his life. It was his first, and hopefully his last combat jump. He didn't know what he would find at Phu Duc Prison.

But he needed to lay his son to rest once and for all. Carmicheal had not shown him the prison roster; he only knew there were supposed to be seventeen American service men held against their will, and, up to now, abandoned by their country.

J.D. touched the rocker that would activate the emergency locator and watched the small LED glow.

The green diode seemed almost white through his NVD. He gently adjusted the riser handles to steer him toward a brighter signal, then clicked the team intercom twice to alert them of the direction change. His team adjusted accordingly as he brought his knees and feet together, tucked in his elbows and chin in preparation for a Parachute Landing Fall.

Each team member pulled hard on the riser handles to flare just above the ground, taking air into their canopies, slowing their descent to make the PLF as gentle as possible. Neither the team, nor the mission could afford a broken, or even a sprained ankle at this point in the venture.

Thuds, exhalations of air, and puffs of red clay dust announced the arrival of Team Bougainvillea on Vietnamese soil. Each member completed his PLF roll, came to his feet in one fluid motion, and began to haul in his canopy.

Chapter Twelve

0130 GMT 5 September
Democratic Peoples Republic of Vietnam

Their 'chutes carefully concealed beneath the lush tropical ground cover, the team headed for the equipment cache, following the flashing flow of the locator LED carried by their commander. *So far, so good. The covert insertion had apparently gone undetected.*

Sergi' Mahoney had stashed the ordinance and equipment in a cave, carved into the mountainside, centuries ago, and well concealed from even the careful observer. The team had some difficulty finding the entrance, even with the locator beacon.

When the foliage was cleared from the mouth of the den, they were surprised by the size of the cavern it revealed. The agreed upon supplies were stacked neatly along the mold covered walls, protected by heavy tarpaulins.

Carmicheal pulled off the tarp from the ugly, yet beautiful, BTR-50. The Soviet, tracked infantry vehicle was heavily armored. As requested it had been mounted with an AK-630 heavy Gatling gun. No markings or identification were visible.

Mike Roberts began checking the electronic detonators, primacord, and C-4. He chuckled his approval as he inhaled the sweet marzipan smell of the foil wrapped blocks of malleable, concentrated explosive. "Out-Fucking-Standing," he decreed as he loaded the Charge Coupled Devices into the bulging pouches strapped to his ALICE harness. "We can blow those little slant eyed, betel nut chewing mother fuckers back to the fucking stone age." The Gunny was clearly back in his natural habitat.

The rest of Team Bougainvillea began loading extra magazines for their '16s and Berettas. Each took a handful of Fog Forming grenades and smoke grenades.

Colonel Carmicheal had elected not to utilize the M3 antipersonnel grenades, fearing that the razor edged, spring steel flachettes produced by the baseball sized bombs would damage his team and the POWs in the close quarters fighting he anticipated.

Carmicheal, Murphy, and Reynolds each looped a one hundred foot coil of gold line around their bodies.

Judd loaded the InfraRed Imaging Unit into the BTR-50. Wade Washington laid it beside the RPO flame weapon, and began familiarizing himself with the controls. Moses Tipton climbed in beside him.

Each team member settled into their assigned role in a feeling of deja-vu. Rehearsals for this mission and a hundred previous missions reactivated the long dormant, combat mental circuits as they prepared for action.

A golden pink mantle spread across the dragon backed mountains separating the PRC from the DPRV as the small band of would-be rescuers settled in to the well concealed cave to await the protective cloak of night fall.

Frank Morningstar and Chad Tanner peered warily through the thick camouflage covering the big C-130, twenty kilometers southwest of Phu Duc prison. *So far, so good.*

0530 GMT, 5 September
flight deck, USS Guadalcanal, South China Sea
Colonel Marcus Biggs and Captain Nathaniel Zelinski shared cups of strong black Navy coffee as they watched the sun rise cautiously from these troubled waters. Neither spoke as they reviewed their respective missions, in the professional warrior's mind they had each cultivated over years of duty to their country. Their single, joint thought concerned, getting those poor bastards out of there. Though neither was certain which poor bastards they were referring to, the rescuers, or the rescued, probably both.

0530 GMT, 5 September
bridge, USS McGowen, South China Sea
The sandy haired Communications Mate First Class handed Major Anthony Wayne a red bordered envelope containing the coded transmission received minutes ago. He was flushed from the dash up the multiple ladders to the bridge and the possibility of some real action. The young seaman had been a part of the peace time Navy his whole enlistment and yearned for the action, the old salts were always talking about. As much as he wanted to hear what the Army puke said to the skipper, discipline prevailed, and he delivered the envelope, followed by a sharp salute, then disappeared down the first of many ladders to his duty station in the bowels of the huge aircraft carrier.

Captain Mortakai Christopher Vacha had commanded the McGowen for the past five years, and had been in the Navy almost thirty years. Though he carried a security clearance of Top Secret, he took three or four discreet steps away from Major Wayne as the aging Ranger opened the crypto envelope.

Mort Vacha had been through both Vietnam, and Desert Storm, and had seen his share of action. He was almost as anxious for relief from the boredom of peace time drills and exercises as was the young seaman. The dichotomy was, a warrior looks forward to war and dreads it simultaneously. He loves war and hates war with the same consummate passion.

"Captain Vacha, the Guadalcannal is on station, these coordinates, please make course corrections to affect a rendezvous at all due speed," The Army Major said formally as he handed the naval commander the decoded message.

"Mortakai! I think were gonna fuckin do it," he exclaimed as he punched the senior officer in the shoulder hard enough to splash coffee onto the burnished decking.

"Very good Major," said Captain Vacha as he reached for the ship's telephone to relay the new bearing to the ship's helmsman and ordered to, "make way at flank speed."

0400 EST, 6 September
The White House

The secure line to the National Command Center jarred Hiram Caldwell from a restless sleep. Judy Caldwell rolled discreetly to her side of the bed to allow her husband a modicum of presidential privacy. Her heart ached for the responsibility on her husband's shoulders. She wished there was some way to help with that burden other than being the figurehead, First Lady. God how she hated that term.

"Mr. President, Lt. Commander Boswell, NCC."

"Go ahead Boz," the PUC replied to his long time friend.

"Team Bougainvillea is on the ground and secure."

Thank God, thought the President.

"Ah Sir, we have information that the NSA may be with them, ah, as part of the team. It's not confirmed, but there is a high degree of confidence in the information."

"JESUS H. FUCKING CHRIST. WHAT THE HELL IS HE DOING? IS HE COMPLETELY OUT OF HIS GODDAMN MIND?" yelled the President.

Robert Boswell waited for his commander's anger to subside, knowing it was more concern than anger.

"Mr. President, we will keep you appraised of any further developments, of course. Also the DPRV have expressed concern over the carrier task force in the South China Sea, as have the Peoples Republic of China. The State Department has informed both governments that the task force constitutes an exercise in international waters."

"Very good Commander," the President replied as he felt for his shoes under the bed. "Thanks Boz, keep me informed."

"Yes Sir, good luck."

Judy Caldwell massaged her spouse's spasming trapezius muscles and waited for him to speak. She knew the current crisis was up close and personal to her man, and it had just become more so.

"That stupid, obnoxious son-of-a-bitch actually went on the mission. He was supposed to handle logistics and supplies, not go to fucking Vietnam."

"Who dear?" she asked tentatively.

"Tom Darrow, my friend, my National Security Advisor. Tom Darrow – Idiot First Class -- that's who."

Judy Caldwell's heart sank, she had known Tom Darrow almost as long as Hiram and felt almost as close. She had shared his pain and grief when his son had been killed in Vietnam, and again when his wife had died of cancer. She also knew that he was her husband's nearest and dearest friend, it would kill him if anything happened to Tom.

1006 EST, 6 September
Washington, D.C.

Clinton Hargrove, senior editor of the Washington Post studied the envelope marked "Personal and Confidential". Post marked D.C., yesterday's date, no return address. The small, precise, carefully looped handwriting looked anal retentive.

He hefted it in his hand, and held it to the desk light. Letter bombs were not an unheard of happening at the often controversial publication, which prided itself on being at the leading edge of the public's right to know and a staunch defender of the literal translation of the first amendment to the Constitution. Single sheet, type written, single spaced, no bulges, wires or opaque areas. The information was, however; explosive:

"To whom it may concern:

"I am a loyal American citizen and hold a high ranking position in the intelligence community. I am speaking with utmost authority, and trust your office to deal with the enclosed information confidentially, and in a way beneficial to the citizenry as a whole, rather than special interest groups and our President's overwhelming ambition.

"At this very moment, an armed invasion is being launched into the Free Democratic Peoples Republic of Vietnam in a ludicrous attempt to rescue nonexistent American Prisoners-of-War. This is without the authority of Congress or the American Public and is in clear violation of the War Powers Act. It calls for immediate impeachment of the President.

"I am without personal ambition or personal vendetta , but feel the American public have a right to know. Do to my sensitive position , I leave it up to the free press to uncover this treasonous act. A citizen."

Clinton Hargrove had been with The Post most of his adult life, and had written may hard stories. He had also served as a Navy Sea Bee in Korea and as a foreign correspondent in Vietnam. He had never met Hiram Caldwell, but admired and respected him. He also admired and respected men who chose to do the hard, dirty chores their country asked them to do. He had seen lives lost in Korea, Vietnam, and throughout the world due to ambitious, unscrupulous reporting by the so called free press. Sometimes he was not proud of his profession, though he felt it was worthwhile and absolutely necessary.

Clinton Hargrove folded the offending document

back into thirds, placed it carefully into the innocuous white business envelope and pulled his battered Zippo from his vest pocket. As he watched the bright yellow flame lick at the edge of the envelope, he stared at the faded crest depicting a bumble bee in flight cradling a Thompson submachine gun, and said, "hang in there amigos – God speed."

"What's up?" asked his comely young assistant as she breezed into the office, two steaming cups of coffee in her finely manicured hands.

She gave him a much appreciated glance down her ample cleavage, as she placed the mugs on the scared mahogany.

"Just another nut case," he answered as the Personal and Confidential letter became so much ashes in the large brass ash tray given him by his former Navy C.O. a life time ago.

0630 local, 6 September
Paris, France

Terry Tanner awoke to the sounds of birds and the smell of fresh baked bread coming through the window of the ambassador's left bank apartment. It had been a long night, full of champagne and love making. *Well sex making anyway,* she thought. She did not disillusion herself that the diplomat was in love with her, nor even that he was making love to her, but *damn, the sex was great.* She had satisfied herself with great sex for years, ever since she had ceased being in love with Chad. Terry wasn't quite sure when that had been. She also wasn't quite sure how many men it had been, but she'd, *made her bed, guess I'll have to lie in it,* she thought as she rolled to press her still supple, firm body against the ambassador's strong back. She felt him stir as her hand caressed his crotch. "Mmm, what a big prick you have," she whispered.

"All the better to fuck you with my dear," he responded.

Chapter Thriteen

0800 local, 6 September
Democratic Peoples Republic of Vietnam

The early morning sun flashed on the edge of the heavy, curved blade as it cleanly severed the head from the deadly Krate before it could strike the Rhade's leg. The Montangyard grinned and nodded his thanks to his commander. Ol' "two-step" almost got him, thought Truk, as he cleaned his blade in the grass. The underbrush concealing Truk's squad size infantry unit was almost as dangerous as the V.C.

Truk had seen the night jump and knew in his heart that it had to be the long awaited American Green Berets.

The mountain people of Annam had fought courageously alongside the American advisors for years, and had continued their fight despite not hearing from their friends and allies in decades. They were, by now, underfed, poorly supplied, under armed, out gunned and out manned. They had continued to fight for a free Vietnam. The Americans had promised re-supply of munitions and food. They had also promised to return. It had been a long wait.

Truk' platoon, originally consisting of forty tribesman had dwindled, over the years to a squad, consisting of twelve aging warriors, armed with captured, ancient AK-47s, though two of the men had the newer AK-74, and Truk carried a prized AKM. He had long since abandoned his treasured CAR-15 as the 5.45mm Soviet ammunition would not chamber in the finely machined U.S. weapon. The Viet Cong, however, had found that American 5.56mm rounds fit quite nicely in the clattering AK. They had also found that the loose tolerances of the Soviet automatic assault rife made the basically inferior weapon less susceptible to mud, moisture, and collateral battle damage.

Truk's men were concealed among the fiery thorns of the wait-a-minute vine watching the cave entrance intently. The rising sun made the sweat run rivulets over the multiple scratches and exacerbated the thorn's irritating sting.

Truk was trying to formulate a safe approach, resisting the dangerous temptation of running, cheering up to the cave. He had to be sure they were Americans, and he had to assure that they knew his small force represented allies. *Better to watch for now*, the battle scared chief decided.

Mike Roberts thought he saw a glint of metal through the foliage. He moved closer to the mouth of the den as he flipped the selector lock on his M-16 to full auto. He made a sweep of the area with his binoculars, then lowered the optics and concentrated with his naked eye. Using the jungle warrior's trick of watching for any irregularity of form or shadow and watching for movement with his peripheral vision. The gunny sat silently concentrating for a full eight minutes by his Chronosport UDT before he decided that the reflection had not been of human origin.

Gettin' jumpy in my old age, he thought as he returned the '16 to safe.

Team Bougainvillea had checked all equipment, reviewed the mission and now awaited the night's mantel. Standing watch was probably the easiest of the two tasks, and each member rotated every four hours. The rest of the team relaxed and ran movies of other missions through their minds, as the synchronized mission clock crawled slowly and relentlessly toward zero hour. Six September was predicted to be quarter moon, and heavily overcast.

Thomas Darrow couched uncomfortably on the diamond plate deck of the BTR-50. Colonel Carmicheal had assigned him the RPO as it took the least amount of skill and training. Judd had also decided that the relative safety of the armored personnel carrier would be the best place for the National Security Advisor of the United States. He had also assigned Tipton and Washington to the tracked vehicle.

Roberts again thought he saw movement in a clump of brush and vines at his nine o'clock position. He lowered the '16 and slipped a curare filled quarrel into the breach of his crossbow. *Let's make this a quiet kill,* he thought as he cocked the weapon.

Truk had made his decision and was about to make his move. Signaling his platoon to stay put, he dug a faded tiger stripe fatigue jacket from his rucksack. It bore the MACV/SOG crest on the right front pocket and the CIDG shoulder patch. Digging once more into the battered ruck, he pulled his most prized possession out, and carefully unwrapped the tattered green beret with the 5th Special Forces/Vietnam flash.

Centering the flash correctly, two finger breaths over his left eyebrow, and crushing the beret down on his thinning, though still jet black hair, the small, leathered man rose from his concealment. He had left all weapons in the brush, and had both hands over his head, as he stepped into the sunlight. If these troops were not who he thought they were, his long fight would end here and now.

What the fuck? thought Mike Roberts as he watched the mountain tribesman walk boldly toward the mouth of Team Bougainvillea's cave. Judd Carmicheal had by now joined him. The colonel hand signaled hold and silence as Truk approached steadfastly.

When the Montangyard had approached within hailing distance, he spoke, in halting English, the words feeling strange on his tongue after so many years.

"Yo! Green Beret! I am Truk, leader of Mike Force Romeo... Please to speak Dai Uy... we are friends... Please no to shoot." He raised his short arms even higher and turned full circle to demonstrate his unarmed status.

"Cover me," Judd told Mike as he edged from concealment. Truk broke into a wide grin and he felt tears streaking his face as he saw the tall American. He had not known this particular Special Forces trooper during the U.S. involvement, but to him, all were same-same.

Judd Carmicheal had made an instant command decision, and decided to trust the Rhade, and welcomed his unit's assistance.

Truk had returned to the wait-a-minutes and gathered his force. They now squatted, together with the Americans in the cavern as the colonel told them of the mission. The Montangyards and the Americans felt as if they were sitting with family. The mutual respect and loyalty had not dimmed over the years.

1600 local, 6 September
Phu Duc Prison, DPRV

Colonel Bat Ky watched the troops of the 325th carefully digging up the antipersonnel mines around the camp. Their commander had decided to replace them all with a new generation of Soviet land mine, and to reposition and expand the entire field. Colonel Ky thought it was a waste of time and equipment. He was also concerned that for the next forty eight to seventy two hours there would be essentially no mine field while the 325th made the transition, and awaited the new ordinance. He decided to place an extra man on each tower and on the fence line during the period. He still had not been advised of the reason for the changes and the extra security, but that was not unusual in the Democratic Peoples Army.

Chapter Fourteen

2045 local, 6 September
Phu Duc Prison, DPRV

The seven men assigned to extra security were snoring loudly on their bamboo mats. The sergeant would wake them in time for their twenty three hundred hour watch.

There had been much grumbling, and more than enough rice beer over supper when the commander's latest whim was announced. The men of the 325th had made good bitching buddies, and they too were dozing contentedly.

Lt. Commander Joshua Bourke wandered through the hills of Pennsylvania with his wife and small son. He could hear his Irish Setter bitch somewhere over the horizon, probably chasing a hapless squirrel or rabbit. The sun was high and the fall colors were dazzling. He could smell water nearby. Yes, it was a good dream; a rare occurrence these past few years.

Manny Rodriquez lay awake, counting the scurrying rats he could hear in the darkness. He could identify at least two adults and half a dozen juveniles by their knawing and scampering. When one neared his motionless left hand, he struck, capturing the squealing rodent. As it's yellowed incisors sought the soft web space between Manny's thumb and index finger, he increased pressure, squeezing the air from the creatures desperate lungs, crushing ribs into it's tiny heart. The rat's companions had run for cover at it's first squeal.

When Private First Class Rodriquez felt the creature go limp, he quickly decapitated it and spat the head across the room, food for it's brothers.

Using his fingers and teeth in the dark, for his world was always dark, he disemboweled and skinned his evening repast. It would supplement the watery soup made from pumpkin rind and maggot infested rice he had been given earlier. Feeling the liver, he could not detect any of the hard nodules that would indicate disease. Taking a smell of the protein rich organ and deciding that it was healthy; he popped it into his mouth. He had to find two opposing teeth that were not crumbling in decay. He savored the slightly acrid taste of the raw meat and the rich, salty taste of the animal's blood. He knew he would survive. "Hasta su lingua in la nagles de su madre! Chavrones!" he cursed into the night.

Major Anthony Flyer tried to peer under the food slot at the bottom of his cage door to identify the source of the shout. He had heard the voice before, but his addled mind could not put a face to it. *Is it time to eat? Maybe a beating? Or a bath?* he thought.

Captain Michael Darrow heard Rodriquez's shout and muttered a quiet affirmation to the heartfelt sentiment. Silently praying that "Goofy" the buck toothed gook assigned to the evening watch would not again beat the little blind Mexican for violation of the sacred silence rule.

There were rats in Darrow's cell also, but he

found he could only stomach raw rodent meat when he was truly desperate. His evening portion of rice had been particularly rich in maggot supplement and that had filled the ache in his gut for another day.

The thirteen other Americans that comprised the inmate population of Phu Duc Prison huddled in the cramped confines of their musky cells in various states of sleep and half sleep marking the passage of another twenty four hours with the monotonous metronome of their impoverished minds.

Their minds were starving not only from the markedly insufficient caloric and vitamin intake, but more severely, from the markedly insufficient intellectual stimulation.

They had all learned the mental calisthenics taught in SEAR school. Most of the POWs had long since finished drawing blueprints for their dream houses, calculated pi to the umpteenth decimal, and recalled as much of the bible as the mind would accept. For most of the abandoned warriors, it was only the unshakable faith in their country combined with the burning hatred of their captors that kept them alive.

Matt Cannon ran his fingers over the pages of a tattered Book of Mormon that had arrived in better days when aviators received Red Cross care packages. The fellow aviator was long since dead and Matt no loner needed a light to read the words of Joseph Smith, as they were burned into his memory. Smith's teaching had sustained him in the belief that a better life was awaiting him.

Colonel Bat Ky sipped his rice wine as he finished his official letter to Hanoi indicating his displeasure of the "un-camaraderie" attitude of the officious little Major who commanded commando unit of the 325th Light Infantry Brigade. He added another line addressing the lack of respect toward a superior officer, let alone a "twice wounded and decorated hero of the 'War of Unification'."

Judd Carmicheal crouched in the underbrush at the edge of the mine field and watched the camp's activity through the eerie green of his Night Vision goggles. Seems quiet.

Mike Roberts was silently moving into a position to fire a bolt from his crossbow into the back of the sentry slouched in tower number one.

The guard in tower number three did not see Dave Reynolds belly crawling through the mine field, probing with his K-Bar for the deadly bombs. Dave's rucksack was packed with C-4, primacord and detonators. If he set off a mine, it would not only make a spectacular fireworks display that would alert every gook within a hundred kilometers; it would vaporize the good doctor.

Judd had ordered Washington, Tipton, and Darrow to stay concealed in the cavern with the BTR-50, it's motor idling and the FLIR active. He had calculated it would take five to six minutes at top speed for the tracked vehicle to traverse the nine kilometers to the prison gate. They were to respond with the full compliment of Montangyards with the first sounds of explosions. There was a fairly clear trail from just below the cave to the main road leading to the camp.

2055 local, 6 September
Vigilant Leader reeducation camp, DPRV

Tran walked his post dejectedly and unenthusiastically. The new political officer from Hanoi had chastised him at a general meeting for his lack of zeal in the on going cause of the revolution. He had also been publicly ridiculed for his "defeatist attitude" when he expressed concern over the breakup of the Soviet Union and the threat from the Peoples Republic of China. He was also told these were not the concerns of a soldier. *Who better than a soldier,* he thought. *We are the ones who have to fight the wars.*

The thirty-odd inmates of Vigilant Leader were all seeking the relative solace of sleep. Tomorrow would be another long day, and there was never any hope that it would be easier than the day before.

2100 local, 6 September
Quang Tri Province, DPRV

Nguen Lo had finished his evening prayers with his family and now lay contentedly with his ear pressed to his wife's swollen abdomen. He could hear his son's heart beating.

Strangely, his thoughts, for the first time in longer than he could remember, were also of the America that had once been his. The thoughts had forced their way, unbidden, into his subconscious for two nights now. Ever since he had heard the sound of a high flying aircraft which seemed dimly familiar.

Chapter Fifteen

2101 local, 6 September
Phu Duc Prison, DPRV
The last conscious thought Le Duc had was of the memory of his young bride's firm golden ass. He was slouched in tower number one, semi-dosing across the DShK, soviet manufactured heavy machine gun. The hollow oak quarrel, loaded with curare, smashed into the young soldiers heart and effectively disabled the 12.7mm weapon.

Mike Roberts moved into firing position on tower number two. The second bolt entered the front of the guard's neck, almost separating the Vietnamese trooper's head from his shoulders. An anguished gasp and spray of blood was all that marked his passing from this earth.

So far, so good, the ex-Marine thought. *Swift, silent, deadly!* Towers number three and number four were dispatched with equal efficiency and stealth. Mike discarded the cross bow and crouched, waiting for the explosions. He had only to wait a few seconds before the first of the blasts rocked the compound. *Shit's in the fan now,* he thought as he thumbed the selector lock on his '16 to full automatic. *ROCK AND ROLL!*

2106 local
Reynolds could not believe he had not found any

active mines in the freshly dug field. *Must be military intelligence,* he thought. Before he could dwell to long on that particular oxymoron, his C-4 began it's orchestrated crescendo down the fence line and guard towers that formed the outer perimeter of the POW camp.

There were suddenly men running in every direction, high pitched monkey chatter screaming distinctive to Vietnamese language, and a boiling inferno of flame and shock waves as secondary explosions erupted.

Dave heard his own voice screaming in his head as he charged toward the cells surrounding the small exercise yard. To his right he heard the distinctive popping of an AK-47, and turned in time to see green tracer rounds stitching the dirt toward his boots

He unleashed a burst in the general direction of the AK's muzzle flash as he felt his left foot torn from under him. He hit the ground hard, rolled to his stomach and let loose a controlled volley at his attacker. He was rewarded by seeing the guard crumple like yesterday's wash.

The guard's panicky shots had only torn the heel from Dave's boot, and perhaps a small portion of his foot. He did not appear to be bleeding badly and the pain was forgotten in the adrenaline surge. *Endorphins are wonderful,* he thought as he again headed for the cells.

The prisoners were all at the bottoms of their cell doors, trying to figure out "what the hell" was going on. Some thought it was the Cambodians attacking, or the Chinese. Not one dared entertain the thought that these might be Americans. There were gooks everywhere, running in all directions, but so far, none had come to check on, or kill, or move any of the POWs. Seems they had been forgotten in the malae as each Vietnamese soldier sought self preservation over duty.

Colonel Bat Ky had not forgotten duty. He ran into the exercise yard and began systematically placing rounds from his prized, East German PPK through the doors of each

American War Criminal. Fortunately, the prisoners' curiosity and the design of the cells collaborated to spare their lives. Bat Ky was firing at precisely occidental heart level.

He had just figured out his error and decided to change clips and begin with the first cell again, when a blast from John Murphy's Squad Automatic Weapon slammed him in the chest. The nine .38 caliber slugs, from the 12 Gauge, 00 Buck rounds tore the colonel's torso from his pelvis. Messy but oh so nice, thought the Sgt./Major as he turned from the bipartite ooze that had been the camp's commander.

The troops of the 325th, in various states of dress and sobriety, tumbled out of their barracks, arms at the ready, just as the BTR-50, answering Judd's radio summons, smashed through the front gates of Phu Duc Prison.

Moses Tipton drove the Infantry Fighting Vehicle straight at the emerging troops. Wade Washington manned the AK-630 Gatling gun and laid down a withering field of fire.

Thomas Darrow used the RPO flame weapon to ignite any errant troops who got within the striking distance of the murderous IFV.

Truk's men poured out the rear ramp of the armored vehicle and sought targets of opportunity.

They had their choice as gooks came at them in all directions.

Judd pulled the pins from the Fog Forming Foam grenades as he neared the first of the cells. The fog effectively filled the exercise yard, giving the BTR and the 'yards some degree of cover.

2112 local, 6 September
nine kilometers from Phu Duc Prison, DPRV

Frank Morningstar and Chad Tanner had rolled the big, black AC-130 Talon out of concealment and onto the tarmac at twenty one hundred hours as per mission time clock. They had just stowed the camouflage netting as they heard the first of the explosions. Nine klicks to the north. They had just began the start up checklist as both uttered a silent prayer to their respective gods.

Engine number three had just began to pop and turn when Chad noticed a jeep turn onto the runway and head toward them. The tongues of flame reaching out from the careening vehicle told him that the occupants were firing at him and his aircraft.

"Bandits on the active runway, I do believe, Chief," he told Morningstar, who had been occupied with checking dials and gauges as the aircraft came alive.

Chad grabbed his M-16 as he extracted his lanky frame from the left hand seat. Frank had all four engines turning and the ponderous craft began an almost imperceptible forward taxi.

Sir Cecil Cedric Tanner III, ESQ. reached the waist door of the aircraft just as the jeep came within range of his 5.56mm assault rifle. He saw that it contained six unfriendly occupants clad in the khaki and pith helmets favored by the Vietnamese Peoples Army. A DShK, mounted on a tripod chattered at the Talon. Big chunks of tarmac erupted as the 12.7mm copper jacketed rounds marched toward Chad.

Just as the driver of the careening jeep spun the wheel hard left to intercept the lumbering transport aircraft, Chad sent a burst into his chest. The overloaded vehicle flipped into the air discarding the soldiers and tearing the heavy machine gun from it's mounting. Methodically, Tanner pumped the remaining founds from his thirty round magazine into the prostrate forms crumpled on the runway.

Chad leaned back against the airframe and keyed the intercom, "Gomers all done, Chief."

"Roger," came the unemotional reply as the plane slowed to a stop. The engines were now turning at idle, awaiting their passengers.

Must be more out of shape than I thought, surmised Tanner as he leaned back and tried to catch his breath. This was the first time he had noticed it was coming in gasps and ominous gurgling sounds. He also had a warm, salty taste in his mouth. When he wiped the spittle from his lips, it surprised him to find it was pink and frothy. It was becoming harder and harder to get air in or out. When the tired English-American let his exhausted head loll forward to his chest, he was astonished to see that most of his chest had been reduced to a red goo, and there seemed to be more air exchange there than through his upper airway. He remembered being knocked from his feet during the brief fire-fight, but had blamed it on Frank's sudden taxi efforts. Closer, tentative inspection with hands already going dead, revealed the awful truth. A 12.7mm, copper jacketed round from the DShK had passed through his right lung, severing much of the essential wiring and plumbing. Sir Cecil Cedrick Tanner III, ESQ. was going to die in a war he nor his country had never fought, and was over long before he died. *Well isn't this a bloody bitch?* was his last conscious thought.

Frank Morningstar was making a careful inspection of his aircraft to ascertain battle damage and it's flyability, when he came upon Chad's body.

"Aw Fuck," he exclaimed to the empty airship.

With a tenderness and respect inherent to his culture, he gently positioned the corpse along a bulkhead in quiet repose. He crossed the arms over the offending chest wound, and closed his friend's eyes. Taking a rough wool blanket from an overhead storage he covered the warrior.

Frank whispered a prayer for a safe voyage across to both the Christian and the ancient gods. Taking the winged sword badge from Chad's beret, he placed the talisman in his upper left pocket, then continued his damage inspection. *There were live soldiers depending on him and his aircraft.*

0916 GMT, 5 September
Orly Hotel, Paris, France

Terry Tanner felt a cold hand grip her stomach. She gasped and leaned forward clutching her slender abdomen. "Ahhh," came her involuntary scream, as she staggered toward the bathroom door.

Steam poured from the shower and the Special Envoy to the United Nations did not notice his paramour's distress. He was singing some sort of dirty Irish ditty at the top of his very mediocre voice, as he tried to recall the name of the woman who had shared his bed last night.

The Special Envoy emerged to find his lovely, little tryst heaving most unpleasantly into the toilet.

"I've - got - to - go, hhh... home," she managed.

"Certainly, my dear, I'll get you a cab back to your hotel, straight away," he replied, anxious to get the sick woman out of his room and no longer feeling in the least bit amorous.

"NO! You pompous ass, I mean HOME, AMERICA, U.S. of FUCKING A.," she replied as she ran a cold cloth over her face and tried to keep her hands from shaking.

"Is something amiss, My dear?" he asked.

"Amiss? Something is wrong, very fucking wrong. Call the Goddamn cab, you ASSHOLE."

Mrs. Cecil Cedrick Tanner III, was on the next plane back to Montana, USA with a cold, sick feeling deep into her very soul.

2115 local, 6 September
Phu Duc Prison, DPRV

The entire prison compound was obscured with FFF, gun smoke, smoke from the multiple fires, and explosions and the red clay Vietnamese dust being churned by the raging battle. Truk and his men huddled around the BTR-50 to give a circle of fire supplementing the RPO and AK-630 as the rest of Team Bougainvillea worked to rescue the POWs.

The ramp of the BTR remained down in anticipation of the POWs. The 'yards had taken heavy casualties, seven of them now lay on the hard diamondplate, uncaring, no longer hurting. Their small, still bodies seemed incongruous alongside the large black Detroit Police Sergeant's mangled form.

Wade Washington had been manning the AK-630 when a trooper from the 325th managed to fire an RPG into the troop compartment. Without a moment's hesitation the large, black cop threw himself on the Rocket Propelled Grenade taking the full brunt of the blast. The muffled explosion had rocked the IFV on it's tracks.

Harrison Chvostek now manned the '630 with a vengeance. Murphy, Roberts, Carmicheal and Reynolds were unlocking the cells, leading the stunned and confused POWs to the relative safety of the Infantry Fighting Vehicle.

There were a few utterances of "What the Fuck?" or "Thank God," but most of the prisoners were to stunned and shocked to more than stare, wide eyed, at their rescuers and follow simple commands. It was a challenge for the team to get them to keep their heads low and stumble to the BTR-50. Judd expected the goomers to send reinforcements, including air support any minute. He was already five minutes longer into the mission clock than planned.

Lt. Commander Bourke was leading Manny Rodriqez toward the waiting tracked vehicle. For once Josh's amputated left foot did not slow him in the least. Manny could hear the IFV's motor running as well as the constant chatter of the heavy Gatling gun interspersed with the reply of small arms fire. "Chinga tu madres, Maricones!" he shouted into the wind as he ran with the Commander.

Major Anthony Flyer stepped from his cell and

marched fully upright into the line of fire of a sixteen year old trooper of the 325th Light Infantry unit of the Peoples Army of Vietnam. The young soldier placed three rounds from his AKM in a well disciplined short burst into the left pocket of the Major's gray tick pajama prison uniform.

John Murphy saw this and rewarded the young guard with a blast from his SAW, neatly decapitating him. John then hoisted the dead major over his broad shoulders in a fireman's carry and double-timed to the IFV. After laying Flyer among the growing stack of dead and wounded, Murphy returned to the cells to check for stragglers or those too weak, or stunned, to move under their own steam.

He found Captain Michael Darrow slumped in the corner of one of the last cells attempting to fashion a tourniquet around the stump of what had once been his right leg. He was trying to use the cloth retrieved from the amputated section. Murphy quickly pulled a real tourniquet and bulky dressing from the field kit attached to his ALICE.

"We're Americans, we've come to take you home," he told Darrow.

"I'll be a son-of-a-bitch," said the POW, the English words sounding strange on his lips and to his ear.

A burst from an AK-74 had severed his leg just above the knee, and he had lost a lot of blood from the spurting femoral artery, but seemed otherwise relatively healthy. Or as healthy as a six foot man can when he weighs barely one hundred pounds. Murphy lifted him easily and jogged to the BTR-50.

Thomas Darrow was still manning the RPO and

did not notice when Dr. Dave Reynolds began ministering to his son's wound. The younger Darrow certainly never looked to see if one of his rescuers could be his father.

Having assured himself that all the cells were in fact empty, Judd Carmicheal signaled his men to load up and Get the Fuck out of Dodge. He had not taken talley, but he knew that his dead and wounded probably outnumbered his undamaged assets. But he did have live American Prisoners-of-War, and he was bringing them home.

Word had reached the DPRV regional command that "indigenous forces" had attacked Phu Duc and a counter offensive was being mounted just as the overloaded BTR-50 stormed out of the prison, headed south. Team Bougainvillea expected to be at the abandoned air strip and the waiting AC-130 in a little under ten minutes. It was now 2122 hrs local time.

Chapter Sixteen

2125 local, 6 September
near Phu Duc Prison, DPRV

The crack of heavy artillery startled Judd Carmicheal from his reverie. He had been taking stock of his situation. The deck of the BTR was awash in blood, the moans of the wounded men were interspersed with the muttering of the stunned, shocked, and confused able bodied POWs.

Colonel Carmicheal joined Chvostek at the open hatch of the Infantry Fighting Vehicle. He was surprised to see not artillery, but electricity crack across the foreboding night sky. His face was pelted by the heavy downpour of a thunderstorm. It was monsoon season in Southeast Asia. The rain felt good. He was old and tired. His sense of elation at finding the POWs alive was tempered by the casualties and the uncertainty of any of them ever reaching "The World".

Colonel Judd Carmicheal, AUS/SF (ABN.) (Ret.)/SAC-DIA (Ret.) made his burst, encrypted transmission to the National Command Center. He was wet and cold and very tired; he did not feel the least bit heroic nor historic. The transmission would probably change the entire history of the Vietnam War.

2131 local, 6 September
Hanoi, Democratic Peoples Republic of Vietnam

Major Nguen Lo My cursed as a curtain of rain obscured his vision across the tarmac. He had just increased the cyclic to lift the nose of his HIND-27 helicopter. He could not even see the other assault helicopters forming his squadron on either side.

The Central Committee had ordered Air Attack Group 457 to aide in the suppression of the "indigenous rebellious forces" attacking Phu Duc Prison. They had been ordered to prevent at all costs, any embarrassing escape of foreign nationals held in captivity. Now the weather was closing in.

Major My had flown the HIND-27 in Afghanistan and knew his attack helicopter was the best ground attack weapon in the world today. He also knew that the current weather made it practically impotent despite sophisticated avionics. This was even more frustrating in that Major My was experiencing that particular problem himself of late.

2130 EST, 5 September
1600 Pennsylvania Ave, Washington, D.C.

Hiram Caldwell had been sitting by the NCC direct line since Zero Hour of the mission. His bladder was protesting the numerous pots of black coffee. He was startled by the jarring shrill of the bright crimson instrument.

"Speak," he commanded as he snatched the receiver from it's cradle.

"Mr. President, Lt. Commander Boswell,"

"Go ahead Boz,"

"Uh Sir, They did it, THEY FUCKING DID IT, standby, I'll play the tape."

Tears streaked unabashedly down the President's weary face as he listened to the scratch voice, now unscrambled, of Judd Carmicheal, bounced off a satellite in geosynchronous orbit. "Homeplate from Bougainvillea, we have live American POWs, say again, we have live American POWs. Situation critical. We have casualties, extraction uncertain, expect heavy resistance, Carmicheal out."

No word on Tom Darrow, the PUS thought as he collapsed in the rocking chair left by JFK so many years ago. *Time to roll the political dice.*

"Boz, on MY AUTHORITY, EXECUTE OPERATION EAGLE."

" YES SIR, MISTER PRESIDENT, " the connection ended.

Hiram Caldwell set with the receiver in his hand listening to the dial tome as he tried to imagine the state of mind of the POWs. *We have to get them out, even if it means another goddamn war,* he thought as he restored the handset to it's cradle. *God help us all.*

2132 local, 6 September
USS Guadalcanal, South China Sea, off the coast of Vietnam

Captain Nathaniel Zelinski was on the bridge when the excited yeoman handed him the red slash bordered envelope containing the priority flash transmission. He grabbed the ICM as he read the terse message, "Colonel Biggs lay up to the bridge, see the Captain," he ordered into the microphone.

Colonel Biggs and Captain Zelinski had adjourned to the Captain's suite and were studying the contents of the classified mission plans which had remained unopened in the Captain's safe awaiting the "Go" order...

Delta Detachment was to proceed, with all due haste to the vicinity of Phu Duc Prison, (coordinates given). They were to rendezvous with Team Bougainvillea, and aide and assist in the recovery of American Nationals.'

The Delta Team was already loaded in the MH-30 helicopters with the rotors turning. A TARCAP of Harrier, VSTOL aircraft, configured for close air support was launched toward the coast of Vietnam.

2133 local, 6 September
USS McGowen, South China Sea,
off the coast of Vietnam

Mort, let's make history," Major Anthony Wayne shouted over the blast of a squadron of F-18/As being launched from the pitching deck of the aircraft carrier. Minutes before, they had retrieved and read their top secret mission orders for "Operation Eagle".

The McGowen had been ordered to provide RESCAP to the AC-130 attempting to egress the DPRV.

The Air Group had also been ordered to provide RESCAP for Wayne's mission. Consequently the various colored jerseys of the deck crew scrambled in a bewildering, but well orchestrated flurry of organized chaos. They were somehow managing to avoid jet exhaust, aircraft, fuel lines, tow vehicles and the surging steam-piston catapult. It seemed a miracle that none of the sailors were blown off the deck, heaving twelve stories above the angry night sea. Nor were any mangled by the four ton war birds hurtling down the short runway at three hundred and fifty knots.

Lt.(Junior Grade) Bradford Rhodes, invariably called "Dusty" by his squadron mates, call sign "Mangler" earned one long evening in Alongopo, was a tall, blond, athletic type who had played semi-pro football for an expansion team of the Miami Dolphins. When it finally dawned on him that he would never make the big screen, he took his engineering degree from the University of Florida had joined Uncle Sam's Navy. Now they let him fly billion dollar jets and roam the planet. *Not a bad life for a single guy. Now it's time to earn my flight pay,* he thought as he scanned the avionics and tugged the harness securing him to his ejection seat one notch tighter. The M-9 Baretta in his shoulder holster weighed heavy on his left chest. The ejection handle between his legs seemed larger and a brighter yellow, and somehow more ominous.

As the blast deflection shield lowered in front of his F-18 Hornet he pushed the throttle to one hundred percent and selected "after burner" detent. Rhodes pushed his helmet firmly into the headrest and waited for the yellow jerseyed CAT Officer to drop his arm. The powerful aircraft strained against it's wheel brakes and the catapult's hook.

When the CAT Officer let his arm fall, Lt.(J.G.) Rhodes felt his body weight increase by a factor of seven as the steam driven piston raced down it's short track, thrusting him and his four ton aircraft toward the sky.

There was a stomach sinking drop off the end of the carrier, before the compressed air near the sea created enough pressure to send the fighter aircraft into the sky.

He was airborne, he thought as the weight lifted

from his chest, and he and his plane, "slipped the surly bounds of earth". Banking into a leftward climb with an almost eighty degree Angle Of Attack, "Tinker 4" joined his flight circling over the carrier.

When all six F-18s had joined on "Tinker One's" lead, the flight headed inland. Commander Ron Preston, "Tinker Lead", had flown in Desert Storm. He had encountered MIG-29s and '34s and successfully evaded SAMs. He knew all three awaited them now. *Maybe it'll be a clean 'swoop and scoop', in and out, no sweat,* he thought. *Fat Chance,* he added.

Major Wayne ran across the wet deck to his team huddled on board the Sea Knight helicopters. The howling wind, and heavy equipment load made the journey treacherous. His mission was to rescue the POWs held at something called Vigilant Leader Reeducation Camp. Military Intelligence felt there were ten to twenty POWs detained there. *Military Intelligence, just like bad pussy, a contradiction in terms,* the Ranger thought as he reached the open hatch of the CH-53.

0700 local, 7 September
GHQ/GRU, Moscow, Russia, UER

Mikhail Gorky watched the sun creep up over thc dingy gray buildings surrounding Red Square, from the central courtyard of the GRU's General Headquarters. He was bound with his back against the blood stained block wall. The September snow seemed fresh and crisp and covered the marks of previous executions at his feet. He watched his breath escape and take form in front of his face. *What a precious thing, this breath,* he thought, almost consciously trying to prevent it's escape from his lungs. As if he could hold on to life, if he could just contain this priceless gas.

The Central Committee had tried and convicted him for treason due to the *release of classified information to an unfriendly nation, injurious to the People.* He had refused the blindfold, wishing to see his beloved Rodina one last time.

Captain Mikhail Gorky was thinking of his wife and children, and his parents, and his childhood home on the Steppes of Russia when the crack of twelve Kalishnikov rifles rang out in the crisp fall air. He did not think of his current mistress as the 5.45mm copper jacketed rounds slammed him against the stone wall and knocked the last of his precious breath from his lungs.

Chapter Seventeen

2131 local, 6 September
abandoned airfield near Phu Duc Prison, DPRV

Frank Morningstar was straining his coal black, intense eyes against the thrashing downpour when he saw the wheezing Soviet APC crash through the brush and onto the pot holed tarmac. He lowered the ramp of the AC-130, and stood on the wheel brakes as he increased the RPM of all four Pratt-Whitney turboprops. There didn't seem to be any gomers close behind.

When he felt the Talon settle under the weight of the loaded BTR-50, a glance into the cargo hold told him they were, indeed, on board. While his left hand flipped the toggle raising the aft ramp, his right reached overhead and slammed the throttles the rest of the way forward to their stops. The ungainly craft actually seemed to leap forward when he released the wheel brakes. As they rolled down the short runway with the heavily loaded aircraft, Frank fired all six Jet Assist Take Off bottles. The JATO rockets affixed to the undercarriage of the '130 provided the extra thrust needed to raise the aircraft off the damaged tarmac. The '130 rotated into the air just as it's wheel neared the end of the tarmac.

"We have shed the surly bounds of earth,"

quoted Morningstar as he watched the jungle canopy pass inches beneath his wheels. Carmicheal and the others felt the reassuring "thunk" as the landing gear settled into it's wells. They were too numb to cheer.

"Bougainvillea Flight, Gold Crown, meet RESCAP on 5576," came the electronic twang over the guard frequency, of the P-3 Orion flying AWACS at fifty thousand feet off the coast of Vietnam. Frank could not believe his ears. *No fucking shit,* he thought as he spun the dials to the requested frequency.

"RESCAP, Bougainvillea Flight, with souls aboard, say your posit'."

"Bougainvillea, Viper Flight with four jump jets eight minutes out. Also six fast movers joining our little excursion into never-never land."

The cavalry coming to save the Indian, the Sioux thought as he clicked his mike in acknowledgment. Judd Carmicheal had monitored the welcome transmission. Now there was cheering.

"Bougainvillea, Gold Crown, we show four bogies approaching your six o'clock at angels three." Before Frank could answer, Viper Lead interjected,

"We'll extend your greetings and salutations."

Morningstar pushed the heavily laden cargo craft for more altitude and speed, while scanning his radar for the pursuing enemy aircraft.

Captain James Wallace, USMC applied left rudder pedal and dropped altitude until he had the flight of HIND-27 gunships on his Air Target Acquisition scope. He assigned each of the enemy choppers a letter designation, and his fellow aviators moved into kill position on their respective target. *Time to visit 'Uncle Ho',* he thought as the diamond moved into the square of the ATA on his Heads Up Display. Then came the sweet growl of acquisition tone. All four Harriers let loose Sidewinder heat seeking missiles within seconds of each other.

The four, small, black dots, barely visible to the Harrier pilots suddenly became small exploding suns low on the horizon.

"Bougainvillea, Viper Leader, Bogies splashed times four."

"Four for the cause," replied Frank.

"Bougainvillea, Gold Crown on strike freq., say your SITREP."

"Fuel four thousand pounds, wounded on board, I think my hydraulics are leaking from small arms fire, controls are sluggish," Frank reported to the AWACS.

"Copy, will have tanker standing by. Come right 275 degrees and head for Dog Golf," the CPO onboard the P-3 advised.

The weary pilot made the necessary course adjustments. He felt very alone in the cockpit and was glad to see Judd climbing out of the BTR.

Carmicheal knelt beside Chad Tanner's body, muttered a curse, and then a prayer. *He would miss the "limey". He would have to look up his family when they got home. He was going to have to look up a lot of families.*

Just as Judd entered the cockpit, the strike frequency squawked again, "Bougainvillea, Gold Crown, you have two fast moving bogies at your 12 o'clock high, angels twenty four, do you copy Tinker Lead?"

"Tinker Flight's hot, Tinker Flight's in," came the quick reply.

The six Hornets swarmed on the patrolling MIG-34s out of the night.

The harsh buzz of the hostile warning sounded in the MIG drivers ears at almost the same instant "Dusty" Rhodes heard the tone of lock-on. The Vietnamese pilots began jinking and diving at the same time releasing both chaff and flares, but their instincts were too slow, and they were severely out gunned and out numbered.

Lt. Don Murdock, USN, watched the pip of his HUD gunsight settle on the high tail of the second MIG as he scissored into position. The Nomex encased finger of his right hand closed on the orange trigger of his flight control almost of it's own volition. He watched in fascination as the tracer rounds from the 20mm armor piercing cannon walked toward the fleeing jet.

The MIG began to tumble, it's control surfaces severely damaged, when Murdock saw the small black figure blast from the fatally damaged aircraft. He saw the oriental pilot's 'chute deploy. "Splash one," he radioed.

Lt. Rhodes missed on his first Sidewinder shot and was lining up for a second try when he heard the heart stopping squeal of missile lock seeking his own hot exhaust.

"FU—," was all he got out as he yanked back on his control, slammed the throttle to the afterburner detent, and popped a flare, hoping to confuse the heat seeking missile. A SAM, fired far below the ensuing dog fight stopped the expletive in the young flyer's throat as his magnificent war machine vaporized. His shipmates watched helplessly. All they could do was make the gomers pay the price.

"Tinker Two, take out that fucking SAM," ordered their leader.

"Tinker Three, let's get the gomer running for home."

Lt. Carl Adams did a wing over and headed for the jungle below. He was pulling five "Gs" while switching his HUD to Ground Target Acquisition. He armed two MK-81 iron bombs as he neared the canopy. He saw one of the flying telephone poles with it's distinctive corkscrew exhaust hurtle past his canopy as he jinked and popped a flare. A sunburst explosion at his three o'clock told him the missile had been successfully avoided.

The gooks on the ground realized their mistake too late. The smart bomb laser guidance system installed on the updated version of the MK-81 had locked onto the fire control radar of the SAM site.

As Adams pulled out of his dive, feeling the release of the two bombs, he was rewarded by multiple explosions on the ground. He also heard the strident buzz of hostile warning. A third MIG-34 emerged from a cumulous cloud bank. Carl watched in horror as 23mm cannon rounds stitched his port wing, throwing him into a diving spiral. The erratic move did cause the MIG to loose cannon lock as the young naval aviator fought to regain control of his fatally damaged aircraft.

"Come on you pig, bring your nose up," Adams cursed as he pulled vainly on the control stick with both hands and every iota of his strength. "G" forces pushed him back into the thin padding of the cockpit seat as the jet corkscrewed toward the jungle floor.

Tinker One and Three were locked on MIG

number two when Tinker One noted his wingman's plight. "Tinker Two EJECT, EJECT, EJECT, GET THE FUCK OUT!"

Lt. Carl Adams could not manage to get to the bright yellow ejection operating lever located between his knees. The twelve "Gs" the spiraling jet was pulling kept his arms locked to his side. He thought he almost had it when his world ended in a blinding explosion. The three thousand pounds of J-4, high octane, aviation fuel sent an oily black mushroom up through the tropical canopy.

Tinker Three had sent two AIM-27 missiles into the second gomer during Adam's emergency. The MIG driver was sent unceremoniously to his ancestors. *Fuck you gook!*

"Bougainvillea, Tinker Lead, splash two."

Knowing there was no need to call SAR for his wingman, Lt. Murdock maneuvered for position on Carl's assassin. Tinker Three joined him, all the while keeping a third eye out for any more surprise visitors. They had not received any threat updates from AWACs.

Realizing his unenviable situation, the last remaining MIG dove for the deck and sought refuge in a narrow canyon. In his desperation he flew the precarious course in full afterburner at Mach three, barely two hundred feet off the ground.

The two Hornet drivers tried to follow his twisting and turning. *Damn this gomer is good,* they both admitted grudgingly as the acquisition tone came and went in nanoseconds. The small diamond danced over their HUDs, never landing on the fleeing black speck long enough for a shot.

In frustration Murdock fired a volley of four AIM-27 heat seeking, Sparrow missiles during a brief acquisition warble.

His teammate had simultaneously unleashed two Sidewinders at the fleeing MIG. They had selected proximity fuse on the missiles and were rewarded by seeing the damaged MIG fly into a canyon wall with an explosion that lit the night sky.

"All Bogies splashed, Bougainvillea, Tinker and Viper Flights will escort you to your 'cow'." Tinker Lead transmitted.

Morningstar acknowledged with two mike clicks. The crew on the Orion cheered uproariously. When the mood settled, the message was relayed to the bridge of the Guadalcanal and the McGowen. Captains Vacha, and Zelinski had ordered the transmission piped through the ship. Hundreds of sailors were cheering, a few were unabashedly crying. All felt a connection with the naval aviators and the POWs. Most were too young to remember the Vietnam War, but most had older brothers, uncles and fathers who had been there. Many had never came home.

2140 local, 6 September
Quang Tri Province, DPRV

Nguen Lo squatted between his wife's trembling thighs. Her contractions had become more regular and stronger after her bag of waters had broken. He could now see the vulva bulging as the small head sought exit from the birth canal. She moaned in relative silence in the stoic manner of her race.

As the small dark head emerged, Nguen gently slowed it's progress and provided downward pressure to prevent an explosive birth and excessive vaginal tearing. As the pressure increased he saw his wife's perineum tear, this child too, would be bigger than the others in the village.

Nguen thought he heard fireworks announce the birth of his son, *how could that be?*

2145 local, 6 September
over the coast of Vietnam

Colonel Marcus Biggs and the men of Delta Detachment had been monitoring the radio traffic from the AC-130 and from the RESCAP. Colonel Biggs switched to the strike frequency, "Bougainvillea, Delta Eagle, understand your SITREP, confirm all assets withdrawn from Poppa Delta, no friendlies on ground?"

Carmicheal snatched the mike from it's cradle,

"That's affirmative Delta Eagle, only bad guys on the ground at site Poppa Delta. Good guys are now feet wet and headed for home."

"See you in the P.X., the Delta commander answered. He had made a decision to divert to the secondary target.

"Snake Eater, Delta, SITREP?" he transmitted on the guard frequency.

Making heloborne assault now, resistance moderate, mostly small arms and light automatic weapons. Caucasians identified on the ground, join the party, the more the merrier," Major Anthony Wayne answered.

Biggs consulted his mission map, then gave the new coordinates to the flight of Pave-Lo assault helicopters.

2130 local, 6 September
outskirts of Vigilant Leader Reeducation Camp, DPRV

The thin cover had slipped off My Ly Tran, who lay naked on the straw mat. Tran admired that special woman curve formed by the swell of the female pelvis. Her pubic hair was matted and still wet from their lovemaking. If the timing was right, he would have another son soon.

Soon he would apply to the Central Committee for a transfer from the monotonous tedium of guarding American War Criminals. Their minds had become so numbed one could not even converse with them. Tran remembered the early days of the Caucasian's captivity. Stimulating conversation was still possible and his English was near perfect. One of the POWs had once told him so.

The monsoon lashed at his simple peasant's hut as he prepared to report for his shift. *A man with seniority, and a hero of the War of Unification should not have to pull night duty,* he thought morosely as he looped an AK-74 over one shoulder and an American made, Light Antitank Weapon over the other.

The driving rain carried with it the distinctive "wop, wop, wop" of approaching rotor craft.

The four, black, unmarked CH-53, Sea Knight helicopters came out of the west, barely clearing the crest of the dragon backed mountains. Two DShK heavy machine guns swung in the dircction of the sound of the turbine engines and twin halogen search lights sought their form.

Captain Robert Brown had only been flying Special Air Operations for three months, but his intensive training and young age fostered a high degree of confidence. He had the twin guard towers pulled up on his FLIR.

Captain Brown toggled the control panel switch

to select an AIM-27 missile from his external rocket pods. He also armed the 20mm cannon mounted in the nose of the Cobra AH-1, gunship. The flight of Sea Knights bearing the Rangers was at his six o'clock position.

Tran closed the hut's door behind him, stealing another quick glance at his naked bride's magnificent rump before fastening the latch.

Tran sought the objects of the searchlight's attention, expecting to see a flight of HIND-27s on night maneuvers. He was startled to see the strange shapes of four Sea Knights with a Cobra in the lead. He recognized them from his Foreign Aircraft Identification course. He could not think of the name, nor the alphanumeric designation, but he did know they were the enemy.

Dropping to one knee, the veteran soldier shouldered the captured LAW and took careful aim. Judging forward speed and altitude was difficult in the artificial light. He took a guess at the appropriate lead on the best silhouetted helicopter. It was the third CH-53 in the formation. The oversized round left the muzzle of the disposable launcher with a thump.

Corporal Tony Parazzo saw the muzzle flash eighty five feet below and was searching for it's source with his NVD goggles when the round penetrated the thin underbelly of the helicopter and detonated. All of his senses were assaulted as the explosion tore his young body into pieces too numerous and too burned to count.

Parazzo was already dead when the chopper crashed into the jungle floor. The fire and explosion killed all aboard.

Captain Brown was aware of his flight's disaster as he locked-on and fired two Sparrow missiles into the first tower. He could see the green tracer rounds from both clamoring DShKs.

A second Sea Knight exploded under the assault of the heavy machine gun still firing from tower number two. Increasing his angle of attack the Snake driver pumped 20mm cannon rounds into the tower. The bamboo structure burst into flames. The Sparrow missiles had turned tower number one into toothpicks, disintegrating it's occupants.

Major Anthony Wayne's assets had been instantly halved. The Cobra was now raking the courtyard with it's 7.62mm mini-guns at seven hundred rounds per minute. The small guard contingency was being rapidly decimated.

As the two remaining Sea Knights settled in the red dust, the team poured from the open hatches and made a bee line for the POW barracks.

Crashing in the door, they found the terrified prisoners crouched around the bamboo walls, which afforded little, if any, protection from the flying lead.

"We are Americans. We have come to take you home," Major Wayne shouted. His pronouncement fell on deaf ears. The inmates sat staring at their countrymen in camouflaged BDUs and Night Vision goggles.

"Let's get the FUCK OUT OF HERE," the Major shouted as he attempted to pull one of the prisoners to his feet.

A burst from an AKM ended the struggle. Both men were cut down. They crumpled to the dirt floor, their blood soaking into the ancient soil.

A hail of 5.56mm fire blasted the guard across

the room. This action galvanized the POWs into action. They struggled to their feet on stiff legs and allowed the Rangers to lead them from their "home".

There was now only sporadic small arms fire as the group reached the courtyard. The airborne troopers carried their commander's body as gently as they could in their haste.

Sergeant Mort Eldridge heard the approaching choppers of Delta Detachment. He was afraid they were gooks until he saw the distinctive shape of the Pave-Los as they settled in on the clay.

Delta Team arrived at the Area of Operations just as the Rangers were loading the bewildered prisoners from Vigilant Leader into the Sea Knights. Two of the Ranger's CH-53s were crashed and burning. The entire compound was littered with oriental and Caucasian bodies.

Too many of them were wearing the striped pajama POW uniforms. Too many were wearing camouflage BDUs.

The Special Forces troops off loaded and began to assist with the mop-up. Most of the POWs were too stunned and confused to do more than numbly stagger in the direction they were led. A few of the Vietnamese guards were still offering token resistance.

Major Biggs saw a Delta trooper drop, clutching his abdomen. Another volley of communist rifle fire killed two more prisoners and a veteran Ranger.

Biggs knew that both Tinker and Viper Flights would be enroute to provide TARCAP/RESCAP as soon as Bougainvillea was safely in international air space.

The Rangers loaded the inmates as well as the

dead and wounded into the various helicopters while Delta Team provided a circle of covering fire. *Everyone goes home today!*

The instant the last neoprene soled combat boot hit the chopper's deck, the pilots slammed the throttles to full military power and twisted the cyclic to it's maximum lift, causing the powerful CH-53s and MH-30s to leap virtually straight up. They were already at one hundred feet over the camp when the locking dogs of the hatches clunked into place.

All seven helicopters, the AH-1 flying as guardian, pointed their noses due west and raced for the relative safety of the South China Sea. The tachometers were red lined as the Army aviators alternated their scan from scope to canopy, searching for pursuing MIGs or HINDs.

Military Intelligence had advised that if they stayed below one hundred and fifty feet altitude, the SAMs would not have time to arm themselves.

Military Intelligence did not think the DPRV had any of the man-portable 'Stinger' missiles. Military Intelligence had forgotten to reckon on a lone, dedicated Vietnamese soldier with a LAW.

The seven helicopters were strung out in parade fashion as they twisted and turned between the razor backed canyons leading to the sea. They were virtually invisible in the night sky, and hopefully were below radar.

All military aircraft carry a plastic coated book titled Operations, usually called "the bible" by the aircrew. It contains schematics and operational parameters for a particular aircraft. In the back of the Ops Manual is a multicolored graph. The white area indicates safe, conservative flying. The yellow bar graph indicates acceptable limits of altitude, and ground speed during combat and other priority situations. The red area was known by pilots as the kill zone.

If your speed and altitude intersected on the red bar, everything had to perform and continue to perform at one hundred and ten percent. The rescue helicopters bearing Operation Eagle and the POWs wound their way through the canyons, well within the kill zone. They were way too low and way too fast. A silent prayer was on all pilot's lips.

Chief Warrant Officer Bradley Abrams Wilson, Army of the United States, had been Army almost twenty seven years. Most of it with Special Forces Aviation Group 144. He had flown the green hats into, and out of Laos, Vietnam, Cambodia, Iran, Grenada and Iraq. He did not bother to pray. He relied on his own ability and experience rather than any divine intervention.

His copilot, W2 Daniel McKinney shouted a warning over the ICM and pulled back hard on the cyclic in a vain attempt to raise the speeding helicopter's nose as the top of a large mahogany tree rushed toward them.

The chopper porpoised and Danny felt his right ankle snap as a piece of mahogany pierced the Plexiglas at his feet.

The thirsty turbojet intake sucked in additional vegetation.

The finely tuned fans chewed themselves up and the transmission froze. This gave the Pave Lo the glide path of a rock. The helicopter and it's precious cargo slammed into the mahogany forest at over a hundred knots per hour.

2200 local, 6 September
DPRV

CWO Wilson gained consciousness painfully. His forehead was gashed. He was sure his left arm was broken. He hurt all over.

A quick survey told him he was still buckled in his armor plated command seat and appeared to be about fifty feet above the jungle floor, perched in the fork of a twisted mango tree. He saw the charred remains of his helicopter approximately seventy five yards from his present position. The sickly sweet smell of burned human flesh, coupled with the offal odor of bowels let go and entrails spilled carried in the jungle to assault his senses.

His copilot, three Delta Team members and six POWs had died instantly, at least he hoped it had been instantly. Brad's stomach contents rose into his mouth and spilled down the front of his sweat soaked flight suit. His left arm had two extra joints and dangled uselessly. Tentatively he tried to move it. The pain was so severe he passed out again.

When Brad came to, seconds, minutes, hours, later, he checked his radial pulse and capillary refill. They seemed to be intact. *That's good. I think?* He decided that the fierce impact must have torn his seat from it's mounting bracket and thrown him through the Plexiglas of his windscreen, hence the forehead laceration and loss of consciousness. He explored the eight inch gash with a cautious finger. *To the skull, bone intact, hell of a headache.* His vision seemed O.K., once he had wiped the blood and dirt from his eyes. *Felt as if he had two 'shiners'. Probably a broken nose.* Blood trickled down his frenulum. *No loose teeth, inside of my mouth tastes like shit, chest O.K., belly O.K., legs, and right arm O.K., neck stiff, but O.K. I think.*

CWO Wilson found the emergency radio with it's built-in, lithium powered, locator beacon in a zippered leg pocket of his flight suit. It had been smashed beyond repair. FUBAR.

The other choppers, along with the Harriers and Hornets should be 'feet wet', he thought despairingly. *I'm sure the crash looked non-survivable. Got to get the fuck out of this tree before the gomers get here.*

The Baretta, 9mm pistol, even with the four extra clips he always carried, offered little security, nor did the Navy Mark One Survival Knife secured to his survival vest. The irony of being shot down over North Vietnam over twenty years after the war ended did not escape him.

2200 local, 6 September
over the Pacific Ocean

Dr. Reynolds had done all he could for Mike Darrow. He gently tapped the elder Darrow on the shoulder. Thomas Darrow had collapsed in exhaustion against the rough bulkhead of the APC. He awoke with a start.

Mr. Darrow, I think there's someone you should see, ah, he's wounded and not in good shape, ah, please Mr. Darrow.

Thomas Darrow knelt beside the wounded POW, wiping away the sweat and grime from the face, not believing his eyes. A vague glimmer of recognition crossed the younger man's face. *Must be delirious*, was his thought.

Tom Darrow saw the little boy who had dressed up in his father's outsized combat utilities to play

"Marine". He was having a hard time focusing through the mist that clouded his vision.

"Hello son, I've come to take you home."

"Daddy?" came the whispered reply through parched lips.

"Yeah Mikey, it's Daddy."

"I love you Dad,' were the last words of Captain Michael Darrow, USAF.

His distraught father, who had come so far and kept the faith so long, cradled his son in his arms and howled like a wounded animal into the hollow of the cargo hold. Many Rodriquez whispered a prayer to the Virgin Mary.

2213 local, 6 September
AC-130 on final approach to Diego Garcia Naval Air Station

John Murphy suddenly felt a vise like grip on his chest and he couldn't seem to breathe. His left arm was numb and heavy also. Dr. Dave Reynolds hurried to his side when he noticed Murphy's ominous ashen appearance. By the time the emergency physician traversed the width of the APC, the Sergeant/Major was pulseless. Dr. Reynolds and Mike Roberts began CPR, but Dave knew the prognosis was hopeless. He barely noticed when the wheels of the Talon touched the tarmac of the American NAS.

2155 EST, 5 September
Department of State, Washington D.C.

"Mr. President, the Democratic Peoples Republic of Vietnam is on the horn. They are raising wholly hell about some type of invasion on their sacred soil," said the harried diplomat to his boss.

Advise them that we lost an aircraft over their sovereign territory during a routine military exercise due to an avionics malfunction and we are currently conducting a rescue operation under international law.

You can further advise them that we are proceeding at all due haste to withdraw any and all American nationals from their soil," The President of the United States replied calmly. He was pleased to note that his hands and voice were now rock steady as he addressed the man from the State Department.

"Sir, the Unified Eurasian Republic sent words of sympathy and understanding and wish to know if they can be of any assistance."

"Send our thanks, but no thanks to the UER," answered the PUS.

2200 EST, 5 September
Situation Room, The White House,
Washington, D.C.

Hiram Caldwell had assembled the members of the Select Committee on the POW/MIA situation as well as members of the intelligence community who had been present at the previous meeting. All in the conference room were silent as they stared intently at the small black speaker phone resting mundanely on the polished mahogany surface of the oval table.

The President seemed smaller than usual, tireder and more crumpled than usual. He had not slept in more than twenty four hours.

The speaker phone came to life. "Mister President, Commander Boswell."

The quiet in the room was deafening as all

present waited for the word from the NCC.

"Go ahead Boz," the President said quietly.

"We have received transmission from CinCPac, Team Bougainvillea landed at Diego Garcia with six live American Prisoners-of-War. Ah, Sir, there were also some casualties, the NSA's son. They have brought home all the bodies. They also brought home seven Montangyard tribesmen who were instrumental in the rescue. We also received word from Colonel Biggs and Major Wayne, Operation Eagle. Delta Detachment diverted to assist elements of the 3rd/75th Rangers of the 82nd. Airborne to liberate prisoners from Vigilant Leader labor camp. Those individuals are enroute Subic Bay, Philippines, there are eight live POWs from that camp."

All in the room set silent for a full three minutes, then a slow applause started, this rose to a thunderous roar. The president wept silently.

About The Author

Gil Hash is a Physician Assistant. He now practices Emergency Medicine in a small hospital in rural Northern Michigan. He is married and has two teenage children.

After completing medical training at the University of Washington and an Emergency Medicine residency at Los Angeles County Hospital, he practiced for a time in rural Wyoming before moving to Henry Ford Hospital in Detroit Michigan.

His hobbies include painting, hunting, golf and volunteer firefighting.

Gil Hash is a Vietnam veteran.

P.O.W is based on the premise that there <u>are</u> live American prisoners of war still being held in captivity in Vietman.

This book details the formation of the "civilian" team composed of former "Special Operations" soldiers through government "plausible deniability", political in-fighting, training and an eventual rescue attempt.

The team members were all actively engaged in various civilian occupations and had "lives of their own" prior to being selected for the team by a former D.I.A. section chief and former M.A.G./S.O.G. Special Forces commander.

P.O.W.

by

Gil Hash

Available at your local bookstore or use this page to order.

❑ 1-896329-01-2: P.O.W. – $4.95 U.S./$6.95 in Canada

Send to: COMMONWEALTH PUBLICATIONS
9764 - 45th Avenue
Edmonton, Alberta, CANADA T6E 5C5

Please send me the items I have checked above. I am enclosing $____________ (please add $2.50 to cover postage and handling). Send check or money order, no cash or C.O.D.'s, please.

Mr./Mrs./Ms.______________________________

Address__________________________________

City/State______________________ Zip___________

Please allow four to six weeks for delivery.
Prices and availability subject to change without notice.